A GIFT HORSE

"I want you to pay me for my horse," Slocum said to the maharajah.

The mahout let out a wordless cry of rage and rushed forward, swinging his hooked stick at Slocum. Slocum deflected the stick with his left arm and reached out with his right hand to clutch the mahout's throat. Gasim's eyes bulged as Slocum squeezed. The mahout tried to twist away but was off balance from his headlong rush. Slocum stepped back, turned, and sent Gasim crashing facedown in the dirt.

Slocum picked up the hooked stick and turned toward the maharajah, who had watched with an amused smile dancing on his lips. Behind the prince, Ali scrambled to get a clean shot without hitting his master. But it wasn't necessary. Slocum grabbed the pole with both hands and broke it with a snap that rang out like a gunshot. He threw the pieces onto the mahout's limp body.

"You fight splendidly," the maharajah said. "I will give you a new horse, but you must agree to be my scout."

JAKE LOGAN

SLOCUM'S SWEET REVENGE

JOVE BOOKS, NEW YORK

THE BERKLEY PUBLISHING GROUP
Published by the Penguin Group
Penguin Group (USA) Inc.
375 Hudson Street, New York, New York 10014, USA
Penguin Group (Canada), 10 Alcorn Avenue, Toronto, Ontario M4V 3B2, Canada
(a division of Pearson Penguin Canada Inc.)
Penguin Books Ltd., 80 Strand, London WC2R 0RL, England
Penguin Group Ireland, 25 St. Stephen's Green, Dublin 2, Ireland (a division of Penguin Books Ltd.)
Penguin Group (Australia), 250 Camberwell Road, Camberwell, Victoria 3124, Australia
(a division of Pearson Australia Group Pty. Ltd.)
Penguin Books India Pvt. Ltd., 11 Community Centre, Panchsheel Park, New Delhi—110 017, India
Penguin Group (NZ), Cnr. Airborne and Rosedale Roads, Albany, Auckland 1310, New Zealand
(a division of Pearson New Zealand Ltd.)
Penguin Books (South Africa) (Pty.) Ltd., 24 Sturdee Avenue, Rosebank, Johannesburg 2196,
South Africa

Penguin Books Ltd., Registered Offices: 80 Strand, London WC2R 0RL, England

SLOCUM'S SWEET REVENGE

A Jove Book / published by arrangement with the author

PRINTING HISTORY
Jove edition / June 2005

Copyright © 2005 by The Berkley Publishing Group.

ISBN: 0-515-13955-6

JOVE®
Jove Books are published by The Berkley Publishing Group,
a division of Penguin Group (USA) Inc.,
375 Hudson Street, New York, New York 10014.
JOVE is a registered trademark of Penguin Group (USA) Inc.
The "J" design is a trademark belonging to Penguin Group (USA) Inc.

PRINTED IN THE UNITED STATES OF AMERICA

10 9 8 7 6 5 4 3 2 1

1

The Grand Tetons rose majestically in front of John Slocum. He wiped sweat from his forehead with his frayed bandanna and took in their soaring purpled beauty after the endless miles of flat Wyoming grasslands he and his traveling companions had crossed in the past week. Spring was turning into summer, and the cool breezes whipping down the tall mountain slopes would be appreciated. If they ever got there.

"You need help?" Slocum called. He craned his neck to see if Hugh Malley could fix whatever trouble he had gotten into this time. Hugh's sweetheart, Darlene, sat in the driver's box of the flatbed wagon and looked peeved at the delay. Slocum shared her irritation, but Darlene had added to the time they had spent on the trail with her insistence on avoiding anything that looked like a ravine, hill or possible rattler den. If things ran smooth as silk and there wasn't anything to complain about, she could make up a new problem at the drop of a hat.

Slocum heaved a sigh. It was Darlene's wagon, not Hugh's. Hugh was a hard-rock miner looking to find a decent job. Slocum had come across them in Central City, Colorado, and had struck up a friendship with Hugh. If he

1

had known Darlene was going to be part of their journey north out of Colorado and then westward diagonally through Wyoming, he might have agreed on some other location closer to Central City.

Darlene was a good-looking woman, but she spent most of her time worrying about things she couldn't change. She tossed her mane of long brunette hair and let the feeble, hot prairie breeze pull it into a small banner proclaiming her gender, as if the well-filled bodice of her gingham dress and the occasional glimpse of her well-turned ankle and calf didn't tell the tale properly. Slocum had to admit he would not have minded a roll in the hay with Darlene, had she not been so firmly attached to Hugh. But that would have been it. To have her nagging and worrying on a permanent basis could wear down any man.

That might be why Hugh had chosen to be a hard-rock miner—he was buried under tons of rock twelve hours a day and only had to worry about firedamp, cave-ins and a dozen other ways of dying quickly. The last thing he would likely hear would be the groaning of timbers or rock crashing downward to crush him, which had to be better than Darlene's constant carping.

"Can't figure what's wrong, John. Can you take a look and see what you can do?"

John hid his irritation as he turned his horse about and walked back to where the right rear wagon wheel had contrived to wedge itself in a deep rut blocked by a large rock.

"We can roll the wagon backward and avoid the rock," Slocum said, seeing the problem right away. He wondered why Hugh hadn't seen this himself. Jumping down, he went to put his shoulder to the wagon to help Hugh.

"Wanted to talk to you, private-like, John," Hugh said in a low voice. "What can I do to quiet her down? Darlene's a fine gal; don't get me wrong, but she never stops flapping her gums."

Slocum knew better than to say a word. Darlene wasn't

his woman, and Hugh had to figure out how to deal with her on his own. Sooner or later it would occur to him that they weren't married, and he would take off to find his own destiny.

"What's holding the two of you together?" asked Slocum.

Hugh braced himself against the wood side and heaved. The wagon came out of the rut and rolled free of the rock blocking the way. The broad-shouldered, heavyset Welsh miner was easily twice as strong as Slocum, but his mind worked slower. Far slower. It took him a few more seconds of laborious thought before he answered.

"She's a bit like my old ma. Think that's it? I want what my pa got?" Then he grinned ear to ear, showing a broken front tooth and another one that had been repaired with bright gold. "And she's mighty good between the sheets. You can't believe the things she can do when she puts her mind to it."

"Don't need to know that," Slocum said. He dusted off his hands and looked at the Grand Tetons glowing a hazy purple in the distance. No matter what, they would go their separate trails in another day or so. He had decided to part company and see what the high country had to offer this summer.

"How far is it to some town?" Darlene called. "We've still got hours and hours of daylight. I don't want to spend any longer on this godforsaken prairie than I have to. I want to sleep in a bed with a fine feather mattress and pillows. How I miss real pillows. Not that your shoulder's not fine, Hugh, dear," she said ingratiatingly.

Slocum mounted and rode west again.

"I'll scout a trail so this doesn't happen again," he said as he passed Darlene, who was hunched over in the driver's box and waiting to get rolling again. "That'll speed up our trip. I think Hoback Junction is only about fifteen miles off."

"Is that Hoback Canyon running to the southeast?" Hugh asked. His eagerness made Slocum wonder what the miner had heard about a gold or silver strike there. But then, Hugh didn't much care what he mined. Coal, lead, silver, it was all the same to him. He actually enjoyed being underground pecking away at the earth's bones to pry loose a few tons of pay dirt, whatever that might be.

Slocum shielded his eyes from the bright Wyoming sun and saw mountains running in that direction. The Grand Tetons loomed ahead, a spine of rock stretching away to the left, towering peaks to the north.

"Could be. It's been more 'n a year since I rode this way, and I don't remember. Anything special there for you?"

"Hoback Junction will be a good place to stay," Darlene said. "It's larger than the rest of those miserable so-called towns we've passed through."

"You been there before?" Slocum asked.

"Why, no, but Hugh has spoken so glowingly of the spot, it has to be far larger than even Central City."

Slocum wasn't so sure but said nothing. It wasn't his place. He spent the rest of the day scouting a trail for them and was about as happy as a man could be when they saw the outskirts of Hoback Junction a little before sundown. Slocum glanced over and saw Hugh and Darlene all lovey-dovey and sitting close to each other in the driver's box. The rest of the world might not even exist.

Slocum looked around for a decent saloon to wet his whistle as they rode down the main street, but he didn't see one. The town probably had a big population of Mormons, who didn't cotton much to others drinking whiskey since it was against their religion. But Slocum had ridden throughout Utah Territory and had always found some establishment serving a nip. He might have to look for it, but it was here. This was too close to Fort Bridger to the south and the Oregon Trail to the north for alcohol not to be a profitable commodity.

"There!" cried Darlene. "A hotel. A nice-looking one. The first since Central City!"

"Go on, get us a couple rooms," Hugh said. "Me and Slocum will poke around to see what jobs're available."

"You mean you want to imbibe liquor," Darlene said in her snippy tone. "Well, go ahead. Get soused. Just don't expect to sleep in the same bed if you come in reeking of demon rum!"

Hugh bent over and whispered for more than a minute. Darlene finally smiled and then gave him a little peck on the cheek. From what Slocum could tell, Hugh was doing just fine keeping her corralled.

The miner jumped to the ground and let Darlene tend the rig. He looked up at Slocum with big brown eyes and a grin that wouldn't quit. "Where's a good watering hole?" he asked.

"See one anywhere?"

"Nope, but there's got to be a place where a nickel'll buy a beer." Hugh was more cheerful than he had been in the month since leaving Central City. Slocum figured that was because he had finally sent Darlene off and was free to get liquored up.

Slocum and Hugh wandered through the streets, politely nodding to the locals and keeping their ears open. Without having to ask, Slocum soon found a street running toward the south of town where there was a bit more coming-and-going than along the other streets in Hoback Junction.

"You got the knack, John. That's only one of the things I like 'bout you," Hugh said, slapping Slocum on the back. The two went into the saloon and looked around. Slocum was used to boisterous singing, bawdy women running around, exposing their privates in an attempt to lure drunks upstairs so they could rob them, or even women barkeeps leaning over to coax their customers into drinking just one more round. This place didn't even have a sign proclaiming its name.

A man with a bushy mustache walked back and forth behind the bar, looking bored. His apron was almost clean, attesting to the lack of work. Seeing Slocum and Hugh Malley lit his face.

"Come on in, gents. I kin tell you got the look of trail dust 'bout you. How's about a shot of whiskey?"

Slocum considered, then shook his head. He dropped a dime on the bar.

"Two beers."

"Comin' up," the barkeep said, not put out by his inability to foist off some of his trade whiskey on the newcomers. He dropped the warm, frothy beers in front of them.

"What's the prospect of minin' jobs around here?" asked Hugh, taking a sip of his beer. From the face he made, Slocum knew it wasn't the best beer west of the Mississippi. He sipped at his own. Bitter.

"Not a whole lot, truth to tell. Most everyone's gone west to the Comstock Lode to paw through them danged rocks." The barkeep tipped his head to one side and studied Hugh. "You look like a miner, not a prospector."

"That I am. My pa and his, too, was hard-rock men from Wales. No coal mine's too deep or ore too hard for me to pick out."

"Save your spiel," the barkeep said. "There's no minin' in the area. Hoback Junction is just that—a crossroads, north-south and east-west. Was, at least."

"What happened?" Slocum wasn't sure he wanted to know, but from Hugh's hangdog look, he needed someone to keep up his end of the conversation. Listening to tall tales told by a bartender was better than Hugh's depression.

"I ain't one to spread gossip, mind you," the barkeep said, and Slocum knew he was the very person to do so. "I heard it with my own ears."

"It?"

"The most mournful sound you ever did hear. Some folks from up Minnesota way claim it's a wendigo. A critter that used to be human but has become an animal, livin' out in the woods and eatin' moss off the north side of trees.

Blood runs from the eyeball sockets! And the wendigo wants to be human again, but he can't. Regular food makes him puke."

"Good thing," Slocum said, reaching over and taking a pickle from a jar on the bar and biting into it. "Leaves that much more food for my friend and me."

"This ain't no yarn," the barkeep insisted. "Half the town's heard the moanin' and cries! Ain't that so, Jethro? Little Pete?"

From the table at the rear of the saloon came mumbled agreement. Slocum paused, wondering what was going on. If the barkeep had been funning them, the other two would have chimed in with even more outrageous claims. Instead, they looked scared.

"At night?" asked Hugh, obviously taken in by the narrative.

"Night, day, 'bout anytime. Strangest echoes all the way from down in Hoback Canyon. Nobody's been brave enough to go find out what's makin' the sound." The bartender lowered his voice, leaned forward and said confidentially, "You get bit by a wendigo and you become one, too. Nobody's stupid enough to tangle with trouble like that."

"Only in Hoback Canyon?" Slocum asked. "Or does it move around?"

"Moves. Last anyone'd heard, the sounds was comin' from up north, in the country this side of the steam vents in the ground. 'Course that was Whiskey Sam what heard it, so nobody's sure whether to believe him or if he was just havin' more of his hallucinations. They get real bad when he don't have enough money for a pint of his pop-skull."

Slocum had traveled through the Yellowstone area many times and had always marveled at the pools of boiling water standing on the ground and the geysers spewing steam far into the air. But anyone living in this part of Wyoming wouldn't mistake the screech of water blasting upward for a tortured soul pissing and moaning.

"You don't look like you're believin' any of it," spoke up a man at the far end of the bar. He hiccupped, then turned his shot glass over so the barkeep could not refill it. Slocum was impressed. Most men kept drinking until they fell over. This one had a sense of when to call it quits. Or so he thought until the man made his offer.

"I'd pay a hunnerd dollars to find out what's makin' them weird noises."

"Put your money where your mouth is, Mr. Glenn," said the barkeep.

"Here it is." The man pulled a fat wallet from his inner coat pocket and counted out a hundred dollars in scrip. Slocum saw Hugh's eyes go wide at so much money. Even though it was only paper money, it was still more than the miner had seen in the past several months.

"What'll it take to collect that?" Hugh licked his lips, then drained his beer.

"Don't," Slocum cautioned. He had seen about every con game played, and this smelled of one.

"What does a man have to do to collect that bounty?" Hugh pulled away when Slocum tried to calm him, to get him to think more before agreeing to something that wasn't likely to pan out.

"Give you ten dollars if you see whatever it is makin' the noise," Glenn said. "All of it if you bring it back alive."

"What if I shoot it and drag its carcass into town?"

Glenn hiccupped, then slammed his hand down on the money.

"All yours, but I get to stuff it and hang its head on the wall in my office."

"What do you do?" Slocum asked.

"Mr. Glenn there, well, he's the town banker. He's worryin' that the noises'll drive off folks. Hasn't so far, but if they keep up, Hoback Junction might end up a ghost town."

"Who keeps the money?" Slocum had no interest in

such a wild goose chase. A wildcat could make mighty
strange sounds. Echoing down a canyon, magnified by distance or altered by peculiarly shaped rock formations, even
the most common of animal noises could sound downright
unusual. If a new steam vent had worked its way to the surface, it might be blowing through rock like a man whistling
for a horse. The steam might be venting through a very
long rock chimney to change the sound. Slocum thought of
a dozen ways odd sounds might be made, and none of them
was worth a hundred dollars to discover.

Hugh Malley thought different.

"I'll find out for you," the miner said.

"Who holds the money?" Slocum refused to let his
friend get swindled, though he couldn't see how it would
happen. Neither Glenn nor anyone else in Hoback Junction
could bilk Hugh out of money he didn't have.

"I'll see to it, 'less you got somebody else in mind," said
the barkeep. "Them boys'll vouch for me. Hell, they'll
vouch for Mr. Glenn. He's a man of his word." The bartender laughed. "Owns damn near most of the town. No
reason for him to cheat you. And he's not the only one who
wants to know what's makin' them noises."

"I'd put up five to find out, too," said one of the men at
the rear of the saloon.

"You don't have that much. Shut yer tater trap," said his
partner.

"I'll do it!"

Slocum motioned for another beer. He paid for Hugh's
second one, also, but his mind was racing. This was as
good a time as any to part company with Hugh and Darlene. They were good people, but the trip across the flat-
lands of Wyoming had drained all the milk of human
kindness from Slocum.

"We want to see what you drag back, mister," the barkeep
said. "Ever'one in town'll want to see. You'll be a hero!"

"And I'll be moving on," Slocum said softly to Hugh.

"You and Darlene can split the money. I think I'll mosey north. Montana is a sight cooler in the summertime than other places. There ought to be enough spreads up there looking for a bronco buster or just a plain old wrangler."

"We can go on this here hunt together, John. The pair of us stand a better chance of runnin' whatever it is to ground and capturin' it. Split the money," Hugh said, but Slocum saw how it was. Hugh Malley thought of this as his new start, his stake, his way of impressing the hell out of Darlene. From the way Hugh and Darlene acted, Slocum could see them getting hitched.

"I'm not thinking of settling down here," Slocum told him. "Let's get a good night's sleep, then go our separate ways in the morning."

"You've been a good partner, John."

Slocum and Hugh shook hands, but Slocum knew Hugh Malley was pleased that he was giving in to wanderlust.

The next morning Hugh headed southeast into Hoback Canyon to hunt for his wendigo, and Slocum cut due north toward Yellowstone.

2

Riding across Wyoming had made Slocum yearn for mountains, really tall mountains like the Grand Tetons. The Front Range of the Rockies was nice, but Slocum preferred the look of these immense, towering peaks. They promised a freedom that no longer existed in Colorado, where settlers and miners were moving in to plow the land and dig endless gopher holes into the once pristine rock.

He sucked in a deep breath and tasted pine and fir and fragrant plants growing in abundance all around him. This was his kind of land, and he had missed it while struggling across the Wyoming prairie with Hugh and Darlene in tow. They were good people, and he had fancied that Darlene had given him the eye more than once, but they weren't the kind of folks who appreciated being on their own. Hugh liked the security of working for some mine owner who sapped all that was valuable from both the ground and the miner, and Darlene sought what she might never find on the frontier: happiness.

Slocum wished he could share his feelings with them. Hugh might decide roaming around above the ground was a better way to live and Darlene could find satisfaction other than in what she bought at some store or what others thought of her.

As he rode, Slocum began to get the uneasy feeling of being watched. The Wind River Reservation wasn't too far off, and he had caught gossip about the Indians not taking kindly to their new land. A few hotheads always snuck away, but seldom did they go on the warpath and do much mischief these days.

But those hotheads might make a bit of a name for themselves if they lifted a solitary traveler's scalp. Slocum felt the back of his neck beginning to itch as he looked around for trouble.

He thought he spotted it, too.

Riding at an angle off the trail did nothing to erase the uneasy sensation that was mounting by the minute. Slocum knew better than to discount these feelings; he had gotten through the war by trusting his instincts, and it was obvious to him now that someone was riding on his back trail. That wasn't too unusual but being unable to spot them certainly was. He was an expert when it came to tracking and hunting—both as hunter and hunted.

He was being hunted now.

Slocum drew rein and sat with his leg curled around the pommel for a spell, waiting for something to happen. The men following him would make a mistake, if they were road agents intent on robbing him. When nobody appeared Slocum knew he had Indians dogging his trail. An outlaw, especially a white man, would be too eager and would never bide his time to strike at the right moment.

Reaching for his rifle, he froze. Movement in the bushes some distance away might have been a breeze he didn't feel where he sat. Slocum left his Winchester in its scabbard and slid his leg back down so he could get his foot into the stirrup. The small movement might have been a fox or even a rabbit, but he didn't think so.

Slocum put his spurs to his horse's flanks and trotted

back toward Hoback Junction, but not far. He cut off the road again, circled and came to a spot where he could get a better view of the bushes that had swayed so suggestively.

A Crow Indian poked his head out and looked around. Not seeing Slocum, he motioned and two more followed. They wore paint, but Slocum wasn't sure what it meant. He wasn't as familiar with the Crows as he was with other tribes. If he had seen a Cheyenne or an Arapaho with paint adorning his face, he would have known if they were celebrating, hunting or on the warpath.

He doubted these three were hunters. Why act so sneaky? They certainly weren't celebrating. That left the least palatable of the choices. Slocum waited for them to move on and try scalping a settler or another pilgrim along the trail.

He cursed under his breath when he saw that they weren't deceived by his circling around to spy on them. Two split from the third and went to the far side of the road, as if to lay an ambush. The third stood his ground, then slowly surveyed the countryside. Slocum stood stock-still, but his horse betrayed him with a nervous whinny.

The brave let out a war whoop and shook his rifle high above his head. He unerringly sighted in on Slocum.

Slocum swung about and galloped off toward the town he had left hours earlier. He knew he could never reach it but wanted to decoy the Indians from his real path. He had no intention of killing his horse with a pointless chase when the trio of Crow must have ponies that were rested and capable of overtaking him before he got halfway to Hoback Junction. He watched carefully, then cut off the road when he came to a rocky patch that afforded him the chance to walk his horse a dozen yards before reaching soft dirt again.

He knew this wouldn't throw the Crow off his trail if they were any kind of trackers, but it gave him another half hour to do what he could to more effectively disappear.

Ducking low he made his way through scrub oak until he reached a stand of pine. The pine needles crushed beneath his feet and released a fragrance that caused him to inhale deeply. He was grateful for the calming effect but more grateful that the needles hid his horse's hoofprints so well. He dodged through the forest until he came to a small creek and followed it higher into the mountains before he reached a point where he was tired and his horse started to stumble from exhaustion.

Slocum figured he had either lost the Crow or left them far enough behind to take a short break. He let his horse gobble knee-high grass at the edge of a small clearing while he ate a cold meal and drank from a stream.

There was no good reason for the Crow to pursue him this long. He had done nothing to them and wasn't likely to ride to the nearest Army fort to tell of off-reservation braves. Slocum lounged back and watched the clouds slip through the intense blue sky. His mind drifted along with the billowing, puffy white clouds until he heard a twig snap.

Like lightning, he swung around. His hand flashed to the ebony handle of the Colt Navy slung in its cross-draw holster. He had the six-shooter aimed, cocked and ready when a Crow brave slowly stood, his rifle pointed at Slocum.

"This looks to be a Mexican standoff," Slocum said. He wasn't sure the brave understood. Then he saw a flash of triumph on the man's face and knew he understood everything perfectly. Slocum was the one who didn't know what was going on.

Without even acknowledging the other two behind him, Slocum lowered the hammer on his six-gun and returned it to its holster. He raised his hands. Let them think he had eyes in the back of his head and saw the two Crow with their rifles trained on him. He saw a flash of what might have been admiration on the face of the Indian before him.

"We're not enemies," Slocum said. "I mean you no harm. I was just passing through."

"Not enemies?" The Crow laughed harshly. "You put us on reservation and starve us!"

"You can share what little I've got in my saddlebags," Slocum said.

"We can take it!" screeched the brave.

Slocum remained calm. If they had intended him harm, the two behind him could have filled him with holes. It had been foolish to rest so long, but he had thought he'd done a better job hiding his trail than he evidently had. Either that or these three were just a tad short of being supernatural in their tracking skills.

"Take that which is offered freely by a friend," Slocum said. "It's yours."

"You can't stop us!"

"I don't want to. I want to share with my new friends."

This confounded the brave. He scowled, then stomped forward. His two companions moved around to flank him. Neither of their rifles left Slocum.

"You are not like the others," said the brave who was doing all the talking. The other two looked at him skeptically. "Why are you here?"

"As I said, just passing through."

"You have heard it?"

This stopped Slocum in his tracks. He didn't know what the Crow meant.

"I have heard many things."

"You will help kill it?"

"What do you mean?" Slocum was at a loss to figure out what the brave meant. "I do not hunt your deer or elk."

The Crow made a dismissive gesture, then pushed down the rifles of the other two braves. They spoke rapidly for almost a minute before turning back to a puzzled John Slocum.

"You listen good, then you help kill."

"All right," Slocum said. "Would you share my food?" He saw the expression on the men's faces. They had spent a good deal of the day on his trail and had not eaten. He went to his saddlebags and took out what food he had stashed for eating on the trail. Slocum decided he could hunt for a rabbit or two in the coming days. The food was better used cementing his friendship with the Indians.

They ate, slowly at first and then voraciously when they saw he wasn't going to stop them. Slocum's entire larder was cleaned out by the time the sky started turning dark.

"It comes now," the one brave said. "It always comes now, when the sun sets."

"What does?" Slocum barely had the words out of his mouth when he heard a mournful sound. At first he thought it was the wind. Then he saw a slight movement in the tall lodge pole pines around him. Whatever it was, this was not a sound born of the wind.

It grew in intensity and was like nothing he had ever heard before. Just when he started to get uneasy, a loud trumpeting sound echoed through the mountains and distance devoured the sound entirely.

All he could do was look at the three frightened Crow warriors and wonder what he had just heard.

3

"Have you seen what makes that sound?" Slocum asked. The three braves shook their heads and looked more scared than ever.

"Let's find out," he said, which caused their eyes to widen. He stared at them for a moment. Here were three young bucks who would go fearlessly into battle and die, if need be, but they wouldn't track down whatever made such an odd sound. In a way he didn't blame them, but his curiosity was running wild.

"Great Spirit not want to be disturbed," said the spokesman for the trio.

"You are good friends," Slocum said, eager to get after whatever had caused such a ruckus. He was beginning to think that the banker in Hoback Junction might not have been amiss to put up a hundred dollar reward for identifying whatever creature made such a noise.

Slocum hoped it was a creature and not a man. There didn't seem to be pain in the trumpeting cry as much as there was challenge.

He rode slowly upslope, leaving the three Crow braves behind him in the gathering dark. As he worked his way through the shadowy forest he heard their horses heading in the opposite direction. Slocum wanted to find a bluff where he could look down and see as much territory as possible.

Within twenty minutes he found a hundred-foot cliff looking over the trail he had ridden before the Crow had begun stalking him. Twilight plunged the trail into inky darkness but Slocum waited, more impatiently than usual, for the moon to poke up above the distant mountains. The lunar light cast a silvery glow over the world, but nowhere did he see anything moving that might have made the peculiar sound he and the Indians had heard.

"Not somebody's drunken nightmare," he allowed. Slocum continued his vigil staring into pitch blackness until his eyelids began to droop and he finally found it impossible to remain alert. He pitched camp, grabbed a quick meal and then spread out his bedroll, thinking that new sounds would probably wake him.

The next thing he knew, dawn was breaking. The night had been as peaceful as any he could remember. But the memory of the booming cry lingered. It was not the product of a drunken imagination, not when he and three Crow braves had heard it, all of them as sober as a preacher on Sunday morning.

He picked his way down the side of the mountain and back onto the main trail, intending to hunt for tracks of something large enough to make such a noise. Slocum had not ridden a mile when his horse stepped on a pile of rocks, stumbled, let out a loud neigh and then tried to rear. He fought to keep his seat. By the time he had settled the horse's jangled nerves, he saw that he wasn't going to do any more riding; the horse was limping badly on a bruised right foreleg.

Disgusted, he dismounted and led the game horse back toward Hoback Junction. It wasn't the end he had envisioned for his hunt. It was close to dusk when he got back into town and stabled his horse, giving the stable boy an extra fifty cents to see that liniment was applied to the sore leg as long as it took for it to get better. Until his horse recovered, Slocum wasn't going anywhere.

"John!" He turned at the call and saw Darlene waving from across the street. "I hoped I'd see you again, John," she said, giving him a quick hug that lasted a fraction of a second longer than was proper for them being in public and all.

"Where's Hugh?" he asked. "Out searching for the noise-maker?"

"He found a hunting party and joined it as a scout. Mr. Glenn said there was no problem if he took another job, if he was the one who solved the mystery. That was certainly a relief since our funds were getting mighty low."

"So he gets paid while he's looking for the critter making the noise?" This had worked out better for Hugh Malley than it had any right to. "I'm glad."

"I don't know how long he'll be gone. Scouting is such arduous work. Look at how much time you spent away from us on the trip from Central City, and that was across mostly flat prairie land."

Slocum didn't bother to tell Darlene he had spent more time on the trail than necessary because he knew they had wanted privacy. He wondered now who it was that the woman was more interested in bedding. She was a handsome woman, not exactly pretty but someone to give a second glance at as a gent walked past. She stood about five-feet-four and had long brunette hair and cat-colored eyes that sparkled like they had gold flecks in them. It was her ready smile and dimples that might have been her best feature, though.

She flashed that smile and showed those dimples now.

"My horse pulled up lame, and I had to return," Slocum explained. "Might be a day or two before the horse can walk again." He knew that the strong liniment might fix the horse up by morning, but somehow that wasn't what Darlene wanted to hear. Slocum found himself more and more interested in finding out what she *did* want.

"We can have some dinner, then," she said almost primly. "I ate at a restaurant down the street this morning, with Hugh, before he rode out to the maharajah's camp."

They went down the street and into the small café to take seats by the window.

"Maharajah?" Slocum asked. He thought he had heard the word before but couldn't rightly place when or where.

"An Indian fellow of some exalted rank. Royalty, I believe."

"Indian? Like a Crow or Cheyenne?"

"No, silly," said Darlene, reaching over and putting her hand familiarly on his. "East India, not like an Indian from these parts. He is a king or something. Royalty."

"Oh," Slocum said. He was more inclined to worry over ordering dinner than he was about some foreigner who had come to Wyoming, probably to bag a buffalo or two to mount on the wall of his far-off palace.

"He is very regal looking. I saw him when Hugh rode out with him this morning. The maharajah gave him a horse, a fine stallion that must be a thoroughbred."

"I prefer quarter horses," Slocum said, working around the chicken and dumplings he had ordered. Trail victuals were all right but nothing matched freshly baked bread and dumplings straight out of the pan.

"Well, it was a fine-looking horse worth a great deal of money, I'm sure."

Slocum and Darlene finished the meal in silence. He started to tell her of his hunt for the creature making the sounds that he and the Crow braves had heard but never quite got around to it. Another sip of coffee or a piece of peach pie, something always got in the way.

Sated, Slocum leaned back and looked at Darlene. She was a good-looking woman, he decided, but he was not the kind to cut in on another man's woman, especially one who was as good a friend as Hugh Malley. Still, from the covetous glances she gave him, he knew what was on her mind. A good meal followed by a tumble in the hay would make the end of the day about perfect.

A sudden tumult outside brought Slocum around to stare through the window.

"That must be your maharajah," he said. A man dressed in what looked like cloth chased with gold thread rode in a magnificent carriage. He was swarthy, with jet-black hair and a long, straight nose. Slocum had never seen that many kings or princes, but this had to be what a prince or maharajah looked like. Fine clothing, the flash of jeweled rings on most of his fingers, a carriage pulled by two prancing white horses, and seated beside him was a woman whose beauty took Slocum's breath away.

"Let's go get a closer look," he said. Slocum fumbled in his shirt pocket and dropped a few greenbacks onto the table and went to the door just as the carriage drew past.

The woman beside the maharajah looked his way. Slocum felt an electric surge pass through him. Then she was gone and Hugh came riding up, waving his hat and howdying with any of the townspeople who would return his greeting.

"John, Darlene!" Hugh bent over and stroked Darlene's cheek before straightening. "Pretty fancy, eh?"

"Malley!" called the maharajah. "Attend, please!"

"Gotta go." Hugh blew Darlene a quick kiss and cantered off to ride alongside the carriage.

"I wish we could have found out more," Darlene said, frowning. "It was rude of the maharajah to order him about like that. He might work for him, but Hugh is certainly not his slave or servant."

"Royalty thinks different," Slocum said, but he had to agree with Darlene. The maharajah wanted to make a big impression more than he wanted to show common courtesy. The Indian potentate descended from his carriage amid retainers bowing and scraping. To Slocum's disgust, Hugh jumped from his horse and similarly bowed as the maharajah passed by.

"Please see to buying the supplies we need," the maharajah ordered Hugh in a haughty voice, then dismissed him with a wave of the hand, which sparkled in the late-evening light from all the gems on his rings.

"Go on, talk to Hugh while he buys the supplies," Slocum said. "I'll see what this gent has to say." Slocum couldn't keep his eyes off the slender woman who descended after the maharajah. Her ebony eyes locked with his again, and Slocum felt the electric tingle once more.

"Wait!" the maharajah called and motioned Hugh to him. They spoke at length, then Hugh reluctantly mounted and rode from town with only a quick, stolen glance over his shoulder at Darlene as he left. The maharajah spoke rapidly in a singsong tongue that sent other servants rushing about to buy the supplies instead of Hugh.

"I wanted to say more than hello to him," Darlene complained.

Slocum and the maharajah stared at each other for a moment, then the man smiled slightly, beckoned to his entourage and walked down the middle of Hoback Junction's main street as if he passed out handfuls of money to the citizens instead of simply smiling at them and saying a few words here and there.

"Please, John. Can you help me see Hugh? This isn't right, the way he chased him off like a naughty boy sent off to bed without his supper."

Slocum said nothing but felt inclined to go along with Darlene. Watching the Indian prince swagger along the main street like he owned it and everyone he saw caused Slocum's hackles to rise. But the sight of the woman accompanying the maharajah caused another portion of Slocum's anatomy to stir.

• • •

"John, are you sure we can get into the camp this way?" asked Darlene. The woman's nervousness increased the closer they got to the maharajah's bivouac outside town. "There must be sentries everywhere."

"I know," Slocum said. He had easily avoided the three men with the thick bushy black beards and the fierce, fanatical eyes. Whatever they looked for, it wasn't a man and woman slipping through the shadows and getting closer to the maharajah's camp. Slocum wouldn't want to tangle with any of the men, but they were ineffective lookouts.

"There's the maharajah's tent," Slocum said. It didn't take much guesswork to figure that out. The tent stood almost fifteen feet high and billowed softly in the late-night wind. The cloth appeared to be something more than the waxed canvas used in most Army tents. The symbols painted on the sides were strange and of unknown significance, but moving inside, silhouetted against the sides, were two people.

Slocum immediately recognized the maharajah. It took a few more seconds to decide that the other dark outline moving slowly back and forth belonged to the woman who had ridden with him. The shadow robbed the woman of her subtle curves and utter, exotic beauty and reduced her to little more than a smudge in the night.

"Where would Hugh be?"

"Servants' quarters," Slocum said. Darlene looked at him sharply, but he was not joking. He pointed to an area near the rope corral. Hugh wouldn't have been hired only to scout, a skill he almost totally lacked. The maharajah would want to get his money's worth and make him tend the horses and any other livestock they had with them.

He guided Darlene through the camp unobserved. She let out a squeal of glee when she saw Hugh sitting on a rock, working away at polishing a harness. Slocum thought it was a strange thing to be doing in the middle of the night but he said nothing.

"Darlin'!" Hugh grabbed his sweetheart and spun her around. "How'd you get here?"

"John brought me," she said. "Why didn't you talk to me back in town?"

"There's a lot I have to say and, well, that maharajah don't like his men lollygaggin' about." Hugh looked over at Slocum and grinned weakly. "He wanted all this here leather shined up before the morning hunt."

"He won't notice, not if he's actually going to hunt," Slocum said. "Buffalo?"

"I think so. I told him there was a herd east of town."

"Is there?" Slocum hadn't seen any trace of buffaloes when they had ridden into Hoback Junction the day before.

"I think so. I was going into Hoback Canyon and felt the ground shaking. That'd be a big herd, wouldn't it?"

Slocum knew herds of buffalo had been counted of upward of several hundred thousand, but not recently, not after the Europeans had taken a fancy to buffalo robes and the hunters had thinned the herds almost to extinction.

"Could be," he allowed. "I'll let the two of you have some time together."

"I can find my way back to town, John," Darlene said, looking at Hugh with admiration in her eyes. Admiration and more than a tad of lust, Slocum saw. He got almost twenty yards off into the woods beyond the maharajah's camp when he heard it again.

It was the same sound he and the Crow braves had heard the night before. Only it was closer. Much closer. Slocum turned slowly and located the noise coming from a draw not a hundred yards away. He touched his six-shooter but decided there was no need for it. Whatever made the sound was too big for a mere six-gun to be of any use.

But Slocum could find out what made the sound.

It came again, grew louder, more insistent. Mingled with it, under its strident call, came a human voice speaking words Slocum could not understand. This time he drew his six-shooter but knew he had a target that would die if he plugged it.

The furor died down and the normal night sounds returned to his sharp ears. He made his way through the darkness with unerring skill and found the ravine where the ruckus emanated. He stared for a moment, then laughed until tears ran down his cheeks. He holstered his Colt Navy and brushed the tears away.

"What is so funny?" came a soft voice from his right. Slocum turned and saw the woman who had ridden with the maharajah standing in shadow and wrapped in a dark brown cloak that completely hid her body. Her eyes sparkled as she stared at him. "Is our elephant so funny that you laugh at him?"

"Folks in these parts think it is a ghost or some Indian spirit."

"Perhaps they are right. We are Hindu and believe in reincarnation. The elephant might be possessed of the spirit of someone from a former life."

"I wouldn't know about that, but elephants are circus creatures," Slocum said. "They shouldn't be the cause of so much commotion. The people in Hoback Junction might take it into their heads to organize a hunt." He knew this was the furthest thing from their minds. The citizens of that fine small town were terrified, but when they found out an elephant made the sounds that frightened them in the middle of the night, they might turn nasty with anger.

"You do not fear the elephant," the woman said. She moved toward Slocum, gliding rather than walking. She stopped a few feet away, and he caught the scent of an exotic perfume. From this distance he got a better look at her face and saw that she wore a bright red dot between her eyes. The thought flashed through his mind that it was like a bull's-eye, but he said nothing.

"You are different from others of this continent we have met."

"My name's John Slocum. You are?" He politely touched the brim of his hat.

"I am called Lakshmi," she said.

"You married to the maharajah fellow?"

She eyed him for a moment, then turned away without answering. Lakshmi stared at the elephant in its pen.

"It is a very powerful beast, but very gentle, unless provoked."

Slocum knew a warning when he heard one. He wondered why she thought it necessary to caution him as she had. Before he could ask, a heavy hand clamped on his shoulder. Slocum turned, his six-shooter half out of its holster as he came around. He recoiled when a knifepoint lightly pricked his belly.

"Ali is my protector," Lakshmi said. She spoke rapidly in Hindi to Ali, who drew back but kept his hand on Slocum's shoulder.

"If he doesn't let go of me, I'll beat him to death with his own arm." Slocum saw Ali react and knew the man spoke English, or at least understood it enough to know he had been threatened. Lakshmi hurriedly spoke. Ali backed off, releasing his grip.

"It is not wise to anger Ali," the woman said. "He is a fierce, formidable enemy."

"Cemeteries are full of the fierce and the formidable," Slocum said.

"You are either very brave or very foolish," Lakshmi said.

"Which do you think?" asked Slocum.

"Foolish," the woman answered without hesitation. She pursed her lips as if pronouncing a death sentence. "Very foolish. Now leave or Ali will feed you to the elephant."

"And here I thought they ate hay and not meat."

Lakshmi turned and stared at him. A tiny smile came to her lips. The smile faded quickly as Ali stepped between them. She drew her heavy cloak around her trim shoulders and drifted silently into the night, Ali following closely. Slocum turned from the impenetrable darkness where Lakshmi had vanished back to the elephant in its pen. He shook his head in disbelief and wondered if the banker might pay him the hundred dollars for discovering what made the strange nocturnal noises.

Slocum shrugged it off. Let Hugh Malley collect his due. He was probably going to earn every penny he made from the haughty maharajah and deserved a bonus for putting up with such insufferable behavior. Slocum fetched his horse and rode back to town, vowing to get back on the trail at first light.

4

Slocum examined his horse's bruised leg and decided it was healed enough to push on. The night before, as he rode back from the maharajah's camp, he had worried that he had thrust the horse back into service too soon, but the valiant roan had not hobbled or even missed a single stride along the trail. Still, Slocum worried. He did not want to be in the middle of nowhere and have the horse break a leg because he had pushed it too far too fast.

"We'll be on the trail soon. No hurry," he said, patting the horse's neck. Slocum tended his gear while the roan fed. He took special care of his two six-shooters, the one he carried slung at his left hip in a cross-draw holster and the other wrapped in oilcloth stashed in his saddlebags. He had learned the value of keeping a second pistol handy back during the war.

Thoughts of blood and death fluttered through his mind. He had ridden with Quantrill and had never been one of the wallflowers when it came to killing. The Raiders would gallop into a Yankee town shooting at anything that moved. Like the others, Slocum had been festooned with six-guns, firing until one emptied and then switching to another and another. He often carried as many as ten six-shooters, which gave him the firepower of an entire squad of soldiers. The rest of Quantrill's Raiders were similarly armed.

Since those days, he had carried only two six-guns and those had served him well, when added to his trusty Winchester.

He was almost finished oiling his rifle and making certain the cartridges fed smoothly into the chamber when he heard a flurry outside the stables. He glanced up to see Darlene looking around wildly. Her hair was in disarray as if she had ridden through a tornado, and her brown eyes were wide and frightened.

"John!" she called. The woman rushed into the stables and grabbed for him. "You've got to help!" She clung to him like she was drowning and he was her only hope for salvation.

"What's wrong?" Darlene wasn't the hysterical sort. She might nag a man to distraction but during the trip from Colorado Slocum had never seen her get anywhere near this upset.

"It's Hugh. He's dead!"

For a moment Slocum stared down at the woman. Her words came as if from a distance and in some foreign tongue he only vaguely understood. Then his mind snapped free and began to work. He had left Darlene in the maharajah's camp with Hugh not twelve hours earlier, and now his friend was dead.

"How'd it happen?" Slocum asked.

"We, you left me, and we went off to—" Darlene turned even paler, and her hands trembled as she lifted a handkerchief to her lips. She sucked in a deep breath, composed herself and started her explanation again. "After we had enjoyed one another's company, I started to leave to return to town when someone called to Hugh."

"Someone? Who was it?"

"I don't know who it was. I never saw him. He was some distance away and barked out the order from behind a tent for Hugh to follow him. Only a couple words. 'Come. Now!' No more'n that. I thought he might have meant someone else since I couldn't see him, but Hugh seemed to know that he was the one being ordered around."

"Was it the maharajah?" Slocum remembered how bossy the Indian prince could be.

"I . . . I honestly cannot say. It rather startled me, and I didn't pay any attention, Hugh and me just having—" Darlene swallowed hard and dabbed at her teary eyes. "I went to ride off when I heard that horrid noise. Hugh had told me it was an elephant. I saw one once back in Illinois at a traveling circus, but never saw the one the maharajah keeps. Until then. After he screamed, I raced to the elephant pen. It was Hugh, but the scream wasn't a word or a call for help. It was just a . . . scream!"

"Did you find him? Hugh?"

"I heard the trumpeting and then one last shriek of pain and rode to the pen where they keep that nasty beast and saw blood and Hugh on the ground and—"

"Calm down," Slocum said. He knew it was difficult for the woman to lose her lover and find his crushed body, but he wanted to get the details. He owed it to Hugh to be certain it was an accident. The way Darlene posed it, Hugh Malley might have been the victim of a murderer in the maharajah's camp. Hugh knew nothing about elephants, and anyone luring him close to the beast could easily have sicced it on him.

"What did you do when you found him?"

"I tried to get someone in their camp to help, but they all ignored me. I rode right back to find you, John. I knew you'd know what to do."

"Come on," Slocum said, taking her by the arm. "We'll tell the marshal and get to the bottom of this."

"I never thought of that," Darlene said in a choked voice. "I'm glad I came to you."

Slocum's mind turned and tumbled as they walked

down the middle of the street hunting for the marshal's office. Hugh might have blundered into the elephant pen and been trampled, but it obviously had happened immediately after someone had called him away from Darlene. That person obviously hadn't stuck around after the elephant did a dance on Hugh's body, which made Slocum mighty suspicious.

"Marshal!" Slocum called out to a weedy-looking man with a dull silver badge pinned on his vest who was sneaking from the office. He looked as if he might have just robbed the place and wanted to escape without being seen. The lawman turned and looked as if he could spit.

"Whadya want?"

"There's been a death out at the Indian maharajah's camp," Slocum said.

"People die all the time," the marshal said. "Ain't no concern o' mine. Undertaker's down the street a ways. Doniphan's his name. Digger Doniphan we call 'im here in town."

"We're not looking to bury him, not right away," Slocum said. "I think he was murdered."

Darlene sobbed a bit harder, and the marshal got the look of a trapped rat. His eyes darted back and forth as if he were hunting for some escape route, only to have Slocum block his retreat.

"What makes ya say a thing like that?"

"Let's go out to the Indian's camp and see firsthand."

"I got work to do here in town," the marshal said.

"Look, Marshal . . ." Slocum waited until the man got the idea and gave him his name. Slocum felt as if he had pried a fleck of gold from drossy rock.

"Rothbottom," the marshal said reluctantly.

"All right, Marshal Rothbottom," Slocum said, his voice taking on an edge. "I'll tend to this matter myself. Might be since you're so busy, you'd want to deputize me so whatever I do is done all legal-like."

"Why'd I go and do a damfool thing like that? I don't know you from Adam."

Slocum moved enough to show the worn butt of his Colt Navy.

"I'm going to find out if Hugh died from an accident or if someone murdered him, like I'm thinking. If I don't ride with a badge on my vest, then I do what I need to do on my own. Hugh Malley was a good friend."

Rothbottom swallowed hard. His Adam's apple bobbed in his scrawny throat like a cork float on a fishing line.

"I'll git my horse." The marshal hurried off without another word.

"What a terrible law officer," Darlene said. She wadded up the handkerchief in her hand, as if she had her fingers wrapped around Rothbottom's throat. Again Slocum found himself sympathizing with the woman, but he knew that force would never get the lawman out to the maharajah's campsite, no matter how satisfying it might be to have his fingers curled around that bony neck.

"Don't expect much from him," Slocum said. He guided Darlene back to the stables. As much as he wanted to protect her from further pain, he had to be sure she pointed out everything in the camp accurately. Slocum figured the marshal would cut and run at the first sign of anything not matching from one telling to the next, and having Darlene there to explain what she had seen stopped the lawman from taking that easy course.

They caught up with Marshal Rothbottom less than a mile down the road. The lawman wasn't making too good a pace, but Slocum found it interesting that Rothbottom knew where the maharajah's camp was and headed straight for it. Nobody else in town seemed to have any idea where the fancy-dressed Indian prince had camped—and they certainly had not known what was causing the odd noises trumpeting through the Grand Tetons and destroying their peaceful slumber.

"How long has the maharajah been in these parts?" Slocum asked.

"Dunno." Rothbottom shrugged narrow shoulders and made a point of staring straight ahead, never meeting Slocum's steely green gaze. As they rode, Slocum sized up the man and found him wanting. The six-shooter riding in the lawman's holster had flecks of rust showing on the metal. The gun would probably blow up from lack of cleaning if he ever tried using it. Worse than this was the marshal's general slovenliness. On the trail a man got mighty dusty and baths might be a week or two apart. That was one reason to go to town—other than saloons and bottles of whiskey and nice cool beers. A bath now and again might even be good for a body. But apparently Rothbottom and soap were distant strangers.

"There's the maharajah," cried Darlene, standing in the stirrups. Her dress fluttered about revealing her ankles and calves, but she was oblivious to such immodesty. She focused completely on the prince and the tight knot of burly men with him. In daylight, Ali appeared even larger than Slocum had thought, towering over his prince by half a head. Ali's shoulders were an ax-handle wide and he stood silently, his dark eyes missing nothing and his powerful arms crossed on his chest.

Slocum saw the twin daggers sheathed at Ali's waist and reckoned the man could use them, in spite of their decorative jeweled hilts.

"Prince," Darlene called, almost falling from horseback in her rush to find out about her sweetheart's death. "The elephant! It stomped on Hugh, Hugh Malley, and—"

"Silence," the maharajah ordered, holding up a mahogany brown hand. No trace of emotion flickered on his face. Slocum decided the prince would be a ferocious card player with such a poker-faced expression.

"What brings you out to my humble encampment, Marshal?" The maharajah bowed slightly in the direction of the skinny lawman.

"This here lady thinks her man got stomped on by yer elephant. That so?"

"Alas, Marshal, it is so. A tragic accident. He was unaccustomed to dealing with such a large creature, and my pet was startled by an unknown man's presence. Perhaps Mr. Malley thought to, what do you call it? Count coup!"

"That's what the Sioux do," Slocum said. The maharajah pretended to confuse Indian war behavior with what a white man might do, thinking it would insult or infuriate him. Slocum had a gut-level feeling that everything said and done was for his benefit, not for the marshal and certainly not for Darlene because of the way the Indian prince had dismissed her earlier questions. "Hugh was called over to the pen by one of your men."

"Which one?" demanded the marshal. "Point the varmint out, and I'll ast him a question 'er two."

Slocum looked at Darlene but knew the answer before he saw her crestfallen expression. She had already told him that she had no idea which of the men in camp had summoned Hugh. It might even have been the maharajah himself.

"She doesn't know," Slocum said, answering for her. Darlene had passed the point where shock possessed her and was now moving on to a building rage that her man had been killed.

"Then there is no point in continuing this inquiry, is there, Marshal?" The maharajah made a shooing motion with his hand and sent his retainers—all but Ali—scuttling away like crabs.

"Don't reckon there is," Rothbottom said. "You want to lug the body on back to Hoback Junction or plant him out here? Like I said, Doniphan's Funeral Parlor's the best we got in town. Only one, truth be told."

Slocum wondered if the marshal got a kickback from each body referred but he said nothing. The marshal grumbled a mite about coming this far for nothing, then touched the brim of his hat politely in the direction of the maharajah and rode off.

"You are free to claim the body," the prince said, "but the condition is rather horrifying to anyone of a gentler persuasion." For the first time, the maharajah made a small bow in Darlene's direction.

"I'll see to it. Where's the elephant that trampled him?"

"Ah, my mahout has taken the animal in question to the lake to bathe."

"Mahout?"

The prince sneered slightly at Slocum's lack of understanding.

"The keeper, trainer, perhaps you might even say rider? No, driver. All of those terms apply."

"Is he the one who called for Hugh to go to the pen?" asked Slocum.

"I know nothing of this. It was a tragic accident and nothing more." The prince cast a sharp look at Slocum, as if accusing him of trying to ensnare with words. That was exactly what Slocum had tried to do, but the maharajah was a slippery character.

Slocum and Darlene rode to where the elephant had been penned. Before they got there Slocum saw the tracks left by the massive beast leading in the direction of the lake, as the prince had said. Slocum wondered if it would be worth the effort to follow the elephant and its mahout, as the maharajah had called him, to the lake. By now any trace of Hugh would be washed away. Slocum wasn't sure what he could have expected to see other than an elephant's bloody foot.

"There's the pen," he said, pointing to a large, muddy section of the meadow where the elephant had been kept. "There's Hugh." Slocum went cold inside when he saw how the elephant had completely crushed his friend. The chest was a gory ruin, but Hugh's face haunted Slocum the most. It was untouched but had the most incredible mask of pain etched on it Slocum had seen this side of an Apache torture session.

"I . . . I'll see to it, John." Darlene looked at him disconsolately. "There's nothing that can be done, is there? The marshal isn't inclined to even ask questions. How do you prove the maharajah knew anything about it?" Tears flowed freely now. "There's nothing to gainsay what the prince said about it being an accident."

Slocum knew Darlene was right. But he refused to let the matter drop.

"Get Hugh back to town. That Doniphan fellow, the undertaker Rothbottom mentioned, ought to do as well as any. I want to turn over a few damp rocks to see what crawls out from under them."

"You will be back, John? For Hugh's service?"

He nodded. What else could he do or say?

Slocum helped the woman wrap Hugh Malley's body in a blanket, then sling it belly-down over the back of a horse from a nearby corral. Slocum didn't bother asking if they could borrow the horse. He suspected the maharajah would consider it worthwhile if all the payment they required to drop inquiries into Hugh's death was the price of a single horse.

"Go on back, Darlene," Slocum said. "I've got a prince to track down."

Darlene slowly walked away, leading the horse with Hugh's body across it. Slocum mounted and picked up the maharajah's trail to see how the prince spent his days. It might mean nothing, but Slocum wasn't so sure.

5

The trail to the lake showed huge hoofprints. The elephant.
Slocum picked up the pace when he found the maharajah's
ornate wagon parked alongside the lake, abandoned. The
prince had ridden from his camp to the lake in his fancy-
ass wagon, which carried more luxuries than most hotels
Slocum had seen west of Denver. A quick glance inside
showed it had been left intentionally. Everything was
placed precisely, as if a servant had made a final effort to
leave it perfectly.

Footprints in the soft earth showed where at least four
people had left the wagon and gone to mount horses.
Slocum frowned, trying to figure out what was going on.
Small footprints might belong to the woman accompanying the maharajah. Lakshmi she had said her name was.
But Slocum could not figure out who rode the horses and if
any of the party rode the elephant. He remembered the
traveling circuses he had seen. The rider had perched on
the head just behind the elephant's ears, using his knees
and feet to kick and steer. One rider Slocum had seen also
carried a pole with a hook on the end of it to poke and prod
the big beast. It had seemed incredible to Slocum that this
was all it took to control the elephant, but the rider—ma-

hout, the prince had named him—didn't even use a bridle or saddle.

Following the tracks was about the simplest thing Slocum had done in ages. The elephant's big footprints were easily the size of a dinner plate. Larger. The immense weight crushed down grass and dirt. As that thought crossed Slocum's mind, he turned a bit colder inside. Such immense weight had also crushed his friend to death. As he rode, Slocum wondered how Darlene was doing. It would take her considerable time to get Hugh's body back to Hoback Junction since she was walking alongside her horse with its grisly burden. He couldn't see her doing the logical thing by mounting behind the body and letting the horse get both of them back to town. She wouldn't want to even touch the corpse.

The valley opened and turned eastward onto a broad prairie. Slocum pulled his hat brim down to shield his eyes and scanned the terrain for some sign of the maharajah's party. Such a large group accompanied by an immense gray elephant could not have vanished as surely as they had.

Slocum continued along the trail but had to work harder now that the knee-high grass began hiding the trail. They had mashed down the grass as they passed through, but it was remarkable how quickly they had come this way. It was as if the maharajah had rushed to this spot for some reason.

A ravine cut across the prairie in the sudden fashion found on the plains. The ground ran directly to the edge, dropped off precipitously, and stretched straight as an arrow eastward. The spring runoff coupled with sudden summer rains shot thousands of gallons of water through here in the blink of an eye.

The gravelly arroyo was dry now. Slocum stood on the bank trying to figure out what had happened. Two of the maharajah's party had ridden down into the ravine for some reason. Their tracks disappeared within a few yards, but he thought they had continued traveling east. The remainder of the horses and the elephant had followed the bank. Slocum wiped sweat from his face, then continued to follow the tracks.

Death came as fast as a lightning strike.

Slocum had ridden out onto a barren plain when he heard the unmistakable thunder of buffaloes stampeding. He swung about and spotted the dust cloud off to his right but couldn't tell how large the herd was or where he might find sanctuary. He knew better than to get into the ravine. His roan, with its still tender leg, could never cross the rocky-bottomed stream in time. Backtrack? Gallop ahead and test the horse's leg? He had to get a better look at the herd's direction before choosing. Guess wrong and he would die.

Slocum knew he couldn't wait too long. The dust cloud obscured the lead buffalo and the sound frightened his horse. Slocum fought to keep the roan from bucking and running. It was as likely to choose wrong as he was.

"Go!" Slocum cried, raking the horse's flanks with his spurs when he caught sight of the buffalo at the head of the herd. He got the roan running at an angle, surging forward in the direction the maharajah had already taken. With a bit of luck, Slocum would reach the edge of the herd and slip away with little danger—if the herd wasn't too large. The buffalo hunters in earlier years had decimated the herds but the buffalo had come back, although not in as great a number.

Head down, racing the wind, Slocum headed across the prairie. His horse's nostrils flared and whites showed around its eyes. Fear lent speed to the roan, and for a brief instant Slocum thought they were going to make it. Then the horse's leg gave way, sending Slocum somersaulting forward. He hit the ground hard, rolled and staggered to his feet, only to lose his balance and crash down hard.

Scrambling, he came to hands and knees, then heaved up, toes digging into the ground to sprint back to the roan.

His horse had stepped in a prairie-dog hole. White bone showed through the flesh. Slocum drew his six-shooter but didn't put the horse out of its frightened misery. The buffalo herd would do that fast enough.

Slocum raised his six-gun, knowing the .36 caliber bullet had no chance at all of bringing down the buffaloes charging toward him, not when hunters used .50 caliber Sharps and had to be superb marksmen. But he couldn't outrun the edge of the herd on foot and was damned if he would simply stand and be kicked to death without putting up some fight.

He fired at the trio of buffaloes that had broken off from the main herd and were racing toward him. He was lucky in one respect. The mass of heaving, snorting, thundering beasts would pass to his right. But what was the difference being trampled by hundreds or only three? They had seen him and in their own frightened run came straight for him.

Slocum saw a long spark blast off one buffalo's horn where his feeble bullet had hit it. In its fear, the buffalo never noticed and plunged on. Slocum stood his ground, firing methodically.

Then he blinked in surprise. The buffalo tumbled to the ground. The one beside it crashed into its hump and fell amid great bellowing. Slocum looked at his Colt Navy and shook his head. It wasn't possible to bring down a buffalo with a handgun. He looked back and saw the third buffalo drop to its knees, then somersault forward because of its great speed. Its body flopped onto the ground and lay twitching.

Slocum had not fired at this buffalo. He was out of ammo.

He heard a new sound over the dwindling roar of the buffalo herd. An elephant crashed through the grass. Slocum turned and saw the huge gray beast emerge from a cloud of brown dust. Riding atop it was the mahout, balanced on the neck immediately behind the ears as Slocum had seen years before. But a large fringed canopy had been added. In this ornate box sat two men, one with a large rifle resting on the edge. Slocum saw the setting sunlight glint off the barrel as the maharajah raised it and silently, arrogantly, acknowledged Slocum's existence.

As the elephant approached, Slocum took the time to reload his six-shooter. He knew now what had spooked the buffalo and caused the stampede that had almost taken his life. The Indian prince was out hunting. From the direction where the herd had begun its mad charge across the prairie rode the rest of the man's party.

The four riders had acted as beaters to get the herd into motion.

"Mr. Slocum, how odd to find you out on the Wyoming grassland at this time of day," the maharajah called. He said something in Hindi. The mahout brought the elephant to a bouncing halt a few yards away, then forced the elephant to its knees so the maharajah could dismount. As the prince did so, he handed his rifle to Ali, who also had been in the elaborately decorated box strapped onto the elephant's back.

"Your men spooked the herd. I could have been killed."

"Why, yes, that is so," said the maharajah. He looked startled when Slocum reared back, intending to deliver a roundhouse punch that would have decked the man. Slocum checked his swing when he saw Ali aiming the heavy hunting rifle at him.

"You are angry. Why is this so?"

"You said it. Your men could have gotten me killed." Slocum looked to where his horse still struggled. He pointedly turned his back on the maharajah, went to his horse and put it out of its misery. Only then did he return. He considered what it would take to similarly put Ali out of his misery but discarded the idea. The maharajah's servant still had the heavy rifle snugged up into his shoulder, ready to defend his master.

Slocum jammed his six-gun back into his cross-draw holster.

"You are angry," the maharajah said, as if the thought had never occurred to him before that any lesser mortal could share such emotions with someone of his exalted rank.

"Almost getting killed for no reason makes me mad. Having to shoot my horse makes me *real* mad," Slocum said, not trying to hide what he felt.

"You ruined the master's hunt," said the elephant wrangler. The man scowled as he tapped the long rod against the palm of his hand. The wicked hook at the end could do a considerable amount of damage to a man in a fight. Slocum wasn't going to let it go that far. If the elephant driver took so much as one step forward, Slocum would drop him with a bullet in his heart. He had reached the end of his patience.

"Be quiet, Gasim," the maharajah said. "He does so like to please me, but sometimes he oversteps his bounds."

"Were you doing the shooting or was he?" Slocum lifted his chin and pointed, Navajo style, at Ali. Ali might have been turned to stone, rifle to his shoulder with his aim directed at Slocum's head.

"He cleans my guns, nothing more. I do the shooting. Have you ever been on a tiger hunt? No, of course not. There are no tigers in this land of yours. Only the wooly buffaloes and other, lesser animals."

"You've never tangled with a grizzly bear," Slocum said.

"A grizzly bear? Why, no. Is it ferocious?"

"It could rip apart your tiger," Slocum said, knowing what a bear could do against a mountain lion. He reckoned a tiger was only a striped cougar.

The maharajah laughed with gusto. "You have such a sense of humor, Mr. Slocum. The tiger is cunning, dangerous, quick, the most difficult of all wild game to hunt. I have lost no fewer than forty beaters and bearers during my tiger hunts. It is a man-killer and a man-eater."

The four riders came up. Slocum was surprised to see Lakshmi rode one of the horses, then remembered the smaller footprints at the lake where the maharajah had probably mounted the elephant for the hunt. Close beside her rode a small, dark, intense man who glared at Slocum. Slocum was beginning to think no one in the maharajah's party cottoned much to him.

The feeling was mutual.

Except for the way Lakshmi kept looking at him. Her servant eyed him like that man-eating tiger the maharajah talked so much about, but her dark eyes held something more pleasant.

"I want you to pay me for my horse," Slocum said. "If your beaters hadn't stampeded the buffalo herd, it would never have galloped across a field where there were so many prairie-dog holes."

The mahout let out a wordless cry of rage and rushed forward, swinging his hooked stick at Slocum. Slocum reacted instinctively. He deflected the vicious stick with his left arm and reached out with his right hand to clutch the mahout's throat. Gasim's eyes bulged as Slocum squeezed. The mahout tried to twist away but was off balance from his headlong rush. Slocum stepped back, turned and sent Gasim crashing facedown into the dirt.

Gasim lay stunned for a moment, then leaped to his feet. This time Slocum's punch was already on the way and connected with the mahout's belly. The elephant wrangler doubled over, his chin in exactly the right position for Slocum to bring up his knee into it. Gasim's head snapped back, and he fell to the ground, out like a light.

Slocum picked up the hooked stick and turned toward the maharajah, who had watched, an amused smile dancing on his lips. For a split second that enjoyment turned to fear when he saw Slocum's expression.

Behind the prince, Ali scrambled to get a clean shot without hitting his master. But it wasn't necessary. Slocum grabbed the pole in both hands and broke it with a snap that rang out like a gunshot. He threw the pieces onto the mahout's limp body.

"You fight splendidly," the maharajah said. "I will give you a new horse, but you must agree to be my scout."

Slocum turned and walked off without a word. It was a long way back to Hoback Junction, but if he kept a steady pace he might make it before noon the next day.

6

It took Slocum longer to get to Hoback Junction than he had thought. Blisters slowed him and he spent two nights under the stars, sleeping with his head propped against his saddle and his blanket pulled around him. Both nights his dreams were haunted by visions of Hugh Malley being stomped on by the huge gray elephant. The maharajah stood off to one side, laughing uproariously. Floating through the dream, though, was the exotically lovely Lakshmi with her beguiling smile and mysterious dark eyes all for Slocum.

He awoke each morning unrested and grumbled more with every step he took. As he finally reached the outskirts of town, he dropped his saddle and went into the cemetery. The new grave in the otherwise desolate graveyard drew him like a magnet. He laughed ruefully when he read the inscription.

Here lies Hugh Malley
A life in mines
Eternity underground

Darlene had a sense of humor he hadn't expected. Then he sobered. It fit Hugh. The man had been from Wales and his entire life was spent in hard-rock mines. Slocum had seen the man's like before. Hugh Malley could talk rock, drilling, mining, anything having to do with being underground like some men talked about women or the big poker hand where they had won enough money to choke a cow. The difference was obvious, though. Hugh knew mining and Slocum had never caught him in an outright tall tale or lie when it came to his abilities as a miner.

Slocum's resolve hardened. Marshal Rothbottom wasn't likely to do anything to bring the maharajah to justice for Hugh's death. Whether the prince was personally responsible mattered less to Slocum than somebody being punished. His hand drifted to the butt of his six-shooter. He wouldn't mind mixing it up with Ali again. Or the mahout, Gasim.

If Slocum had to pick a place to start asking his hard questions, it would be with Gasim. The elephant driver was unpleasant, but Slocum had seen any number of good-hearted men who acted liked jackasses. He had the gut feeling Gasim had showed his true face when he had attacked with the hooked staff.

Slocum left Hugh's grave with a silent vow to plant the man's killer in the same cemetery, hefted his gear and walked the remaining mile to town. Dusk gave Hoback Junction softer edges, and the gaslights hadn't been turned on yet. Slocum dropped his saddle and sat on it, watching the sun set over the Grand Tetons. Such beauty mixed with ugly death—that summed up the way Slocum looked at the world.

"John?"

He glanced over his shoulder to see Darlene behind him. He had not heard her come up since he had been lost in thought.

"I saw Hugh's grave. You did good putting that marker on it. Hugh'd like it."

"Thank you. It took 'bout all my money, but he deserved

it." Darlene looked around at the bustle of the townspeople and heaved a deep sigh. From that angle, Slocum got a good view of her breasts rising and falling under her somewhat dirtied blouse. She turned and set her skirt whirling around. Slocum stood quickly to keep himself from getting distracted even more by her feminine charms.

"I'm about tapped out, too," Slocum said. He did not bother going into the story of how he had lost his horse. Getting another, even if he could find one with as stout a heart, would cost a fabulous amount of money. Maybe a hundred dollars since this was a frontier town willing to bilk anyone passing through.

Darlene turned and looked at him with a soft, unfocused stare.

"We should team up," she said. It was clear to Slocum what she meant. Darlene was a good-looking woman, but Slocum wasn't sure he wanted to take up with the sweetheart of a dead friend. She was more likely to be seeking out anyone to cling to, to take care of her, to lean on because Hugh was gone. Slocum didn't want that kind of attachment from her because it would be for all the wrong reasons.

"Hugh has to be avenged," both of them said at the same time.

Slocum looked at her and then laughed. Darlene did think a lot like him. That wasn't necessarily a good thing. Or was it?

"I've got a hotel room for one more night," she said. "Gets mighty lonely in that big bed without Hugh."

"Darlene—" he started.

"John, I don't want anything from you. Nothing but a night where I can forget Hugh. For a spell. In the morning we can go our separate ways."

"Or maybe we can figure out how to get some justice for Hugh," he said.

"I want that," she said. "As much as I want you. Now."

Darlene moved closer and looked up at him. For a moment Slocum thought she was going to violate all the laws about public decency and kiss him, but she stopped an inch shy. He felt her hot breath and soaked up some of the heat from her body.

Slocum stepped back. Darlene caught her breath, then let it out in a sigh of relief when he stooped to pick up his gear and came back to her. Side by side they went to the hotel without saying another word and trooped up the rickety stairs. The second floor was full. So was the third. Darlene had a tiny room crammed in under the sloping roof on the fourth floor. The big bed she had mentioned was hardly wide enough for one person, but Slocum doubted they would be doing much sleeping.

"Drop your saddle over there," Darlene said, pointing to a small chest where guests could store their clothing. She moved closer and boldly said, "And drop your pants here."

Slocum heaved his saddle to the top of the chest. By the time it crashed down, Darlene was already working on his jeans. As she opened the buttons on his fly one by one, he carefully unfastened the buckle on his gun belt and laid it aside.

"So big," she cooed, reaching into the fly and teasing out the thick shaft, which had been hidden away for too long. Darlene moved even closer and brushed her lips across the underside of his fleshy rod. Then she made a giant gulping sound and devoured him totally. Slocum's knees went weak as he reached down to run his fingers through her dark hair to balance himself.

"Go on, stroke my hair. I like that," Darlene said, pulling away from him for a moment. She returned immediately, kissing, licking and then gently sucking on the thick tip that bobbed about harder and bigger with every feathery touch of her mouth.

Slocum did as she asked, his fingers moving over the thick strands of her soft, long hair. Every time he stroked back, Darlene moved her head forward and took a little more of him into her mouth. Slocum quickly got the idea and began guiding her in the motion he liked most by the way he ran his fingers over and through her thick locks.

A slurping sound filled the tiny room and worked even more erotic magic on Slocum. He had wondered, now and then while they were all out on the trail, what Darlene might be like, but he had not dwelled too much on such fantasies since she and Hugh had been together, and Hugh Malley had been a friend.

The thought crossed Slocum's mind that this wasn't the right way to honor the man's memory and then vanished for good. Hugh was dead and buried. Whatever fleshy bond Hugh and she had before was now gone. Darlene needed him now as much as he needed her. It was a good trade.

Darlene gobbled and sucked and licked until Slocum's knees began to sag. His legs turned watery as sensations rippled throughout his loins, and he knew he was not going to withstand much more of the woman's oral assault.

Slocum turned slowly, letting Darlene come along with him. Then he sat on the edge of the bed. Darlene looked up. Her eyes turned up to look at him. Slocum saw gold flecks in those eyes. He knew he had hit the mother lode by the way Darlene worked so avidly.

"You're so big," Darlene said again, her fingers curling and uncurling around his steely stalk.

Slocum did not answer with words. Instead, he reached down and took her shoulders, gently drawing her to her feet. Darlene was much shorter but now towered over the seated Slocum. Looking straight ahead, he could see bare flesh poking through the single gap in her blouse just above her navel. He began working on her blouse to get the buttons free to expose more of her luscious skin. He did not work quickly enough for her. Darlene helped with the tiny pearl buttons and quickly revealed the naked swells of her firm breasts. The coral tips were surrounded by brownish, bumpy plains that drew Slocum's mouth as surely as Darlene's had found their target at his crotch.

Slocum licked from the underside all the way to the top of each breast in turn. Darlene purred like a contented cat and arched her back, trying to get more of her succulent flesh into his mouth. Slocum teased her with the promise of more, only to draw back and do something else.

He kissed those rock-hard nubs cresting each mound of snowy flesh, only to kiss his way to the deep valley when she tried to shove her chest forward and let his mouth engulf her tender flesh.

He toyed with her nipples, then suddenly spun the woman about. Darlene let out a cry of surprise and reached out, catching herself on the cedar chest where she had stored her clothing.

Bent over, her behind jutting up into the air, Darlene gasped with joy when Slocum ran his hands up under her skirts. His hands found her sleek legs and worked quickly up to her naked thighs. Slocum's hands parted those thighs and then he hiked her skirts up around her waist to expose her bare hindquarters.

"You don't wear any of those frilly undies most ladies prefer," Slocum said.

"Does that bother you?" She looked back over her shoulder as she braced herself on the chest. Darlene widened her stance enough to emphasize what sort of answer she wanted to hear.

"It excites me."

Slocum showed her how much. He bunched her skirts around her waist and stroked over the smooth curves of her rump. The flesh trembled at his touch. He ran his hand faster and faster over her naked cheeks until he felt friction building.

"I . . . I'm getting so hot, John. And damp inside. I—" Darlene let out a yelp as Slocum lightly spanked her bottom. He continued to spank until her hindquarters were a rosy red and she sagged forward, half lying across the chest.

Then he moved into position. Slocum pushed down his pants around his ankles and kicked free, stood and placed his hands on her flaring hips. Before Darlene could say a word, Slocum's hips spoke for them both. He slid forward, the chunky tip of his manhood bouncing along the woman's nether lips. The pinkly scalloped gates protecting her innermost secrets fluttered gently and then opened to the fleshy invader.

Slocum slid fully into her.

For a moment, the world spun around him. He caught his breath and savored the intense sensations rampaging throughout his loins. The warmth that surrounded him became more intense. Then Darlene gasped. Slocum felt as if a gloved hand tightened around his manhood. She gasped and moaned and then sighed.

"So nice, John. I . . . I didn't know it could be like this."

"It won't be for long," Slocum said. "It'll get better."

Slocum began moving with deliberate speed. Deeper into her gently yielding body, then an agonizingly slow retreat that built both their desires to the breaking point. Slocum hesitated as he stayed between the fleshy curtains of her most intimate recess, then he plunged back with more speed. The friction that he had built using his hands across her rounded bottom now magnified internally as he slid with assurance ever deeper into her body.

Darlene began bucking and thrashing about, impaled on his thickness. Slocum reached down and caught her around the waist to keep her from inadvertently escaping. He pushed forward and braced her upper legs against the chest. Darlene sprawled forward so her breasts were flattened across the wooden lid of the chest, and she grasped the far side to keep from slipping to one side. When

Slocum felt this new buttressing, he began thrusting with more power, trying to bury himself even deeper within her.

Darlene shrieked with uncontrollable pleasure as the tension mounted. Her hips began moving in quick, tight circles and then pushed back to fit perfectly into the circle of his groin as she silently begged for more. Slocum was the man to let her have it. He knew he could go on a bit longer. But not much. The way she sounded, the way she felt, the way she responded so powerfully took its toll on his control. Slocum began to lose control and then all restraint fled. Hips flying like a shuttlecock, he sank faster and faster into Darlene's yearning interior. Her molten center welcomed him eagerly, cradled him tenderly, massaged his entire length as it slipped back and forth and then crushed him as a new wave of desire washed through her body.

Slocum felt the fiery tide rising within and then lost all control. A roaring in his ears blotted out Darlene's new cries of ecstasy.

Slocum held Darlene's hips for a moment longer, then fell back and sat on the edge of the bed. She sank to her knees, then swiveled about to sit cross-legged on the floor to stare at him. She was flushed. Her cheeks were as rosy as the ones he had spanked and her eyes blazed with erotic fire.

"More," she said breathlessly. "I want more. It's never been this good."

Slocum was willing, but it took a spell for him to do much about it. He found it a mite restrictive making love in the bed since the ceiling sloped down so low, but as he had always been told, where there's a will there's a way.

He had the will and he found the way, much to their mutual delight.

7

Slocum's eyelids flickered open, and for a moment he thought he had been tossed into a bramble bush. He pulled back and saw he was staring at the back of Darlene's dark-haired head. The short hairs on her neck looked spiky this close. He edged away, then got out of the bed, careful not to bang his head against the sloping ceiling. He pulled on his pants, then got into the rest of his clothes. He finished buckling on his gun belt before the woman awoke.

"John?" She rolled over in bed and let the sheet fall away from her chest to reveal the twin glories he had so delighted in the night before. "Where are you going?"

Slocum started to answer but realized he didn't have a good answer for her. He sat on the cedar chest and looked at her as a shaft of morning sunlight slanted in through the narrow window mounted at the top of the room. It was as if she were a performer on stage caught in a spotlight.

"I don't know. I have to get some money. There must be a job going wanting around town," he said.

"What about Hugh? You can't let him lie uneasy in his grave. Somebody in the maharajah's camp killed him. I'm sure of it. He was murdered!"

"I know," Slocum said. If a woman had told him the details of Hugh Malley's death without him personally seeing that it was all true, he would have thought she was hysterical. But Slocum knew. Ali might have done the killing or, more likely, the mahout, Gasim. He couldn't even discount that they were all involved.

He believed the maharajah knew of the death and had brushed it off. Whether the Indian prince had ordered Hugh's death was something Slocum intended to find out. It didn't matter that much to Slocum if the maharajah and his servants were all strung up—or ended their miserable lives with bullets in them—if they were guilty of Hugh's death.

"I can get a job, John. I know how to do all kinds of things."

"I know," Slocum said, grinning.

Darlene blushed and chastely drew up the sheet to hide what Slocum had already seen.

"I didn't mean that. I'm not that kind of girl. I've worked in stores. I kept books at a bank. I've even cooked for an entire crew of cowboys on a ranch, though I wasn't anywhere near as good as the regular chuck wagon cook."

"That's fine," Slocum said. He was glad Darlene could get along without Hugh, though he wondered because of the way she had clung so to the miner as if he were her only hope of survival. Slocum had to consider that Darlene and Hugh had been in love. That made her desire to see Hugh's killer brought to justice all the more important.

"You're skeptical. I can earn enough—honestly—to get you a new horse. Then it's up to you."

"A horse is a mighty expensive proposition," Slocum said. "It'd take too long to save that kind of money, what with the need to live off what you make along the way." His mind turned over everything and came up with only one possible way of finding Hugh's killer. It didn't suit him much, but he had done worse in his life. Much worse.

"So what do your propose to do?" Darlene turned indignant now that she thought he was going to steal a horse and simply ride out of Hoback Junction without bringing Hugh's killer to justice.

"Get your job," Slocum said, "and I'll take one that's already been offered to me."

"Much obliged for the ride," Slocum said to the wagon driver. The young man worked at the Hoback Junction general store and brought fresh supplies to the maharajah's camp every other day. In return for helping load and unload, Slocum had avoided walking back to the prince's campsite with his saddle balanced on his shoulder.

"You want a job, Slocum, and I'll see that Mr. Gutherie hires you on. We kin sure use the extra help these days."

"Got a job here," Slocum said, looking at the ornate tents gently flapping in the fitful prairie wind. Nobody stirred in the camp, but it was late afternoon. If the Indian prince and his servants had any sense, they'd follow the Mexican custom of a siesta during the hottest part of the day.

Slocum saw that they didn't have that kind of sense. The maharajah, seated in his fancy carriage, drove toward the camp from an obviously long trip across the Wyoming grasslands. Slocum didn't see any large caliber rifles so he figured the maharajah had been hunting something other than buffalo. Or maybe he had just been sightseeing.

As the carriage drew closer, Slocum saw Lakshmi seated behind the prince and Ali, who drove. Her servant sat stoically in the rear of the carriage, eating dust kicked up by the large wheels and struggling hard not to show any discomfort.

Ali pulled back cruelly hard on the reins and stopped the carriage a few yards from Slocum. The prince jumped lightly to the ground and strutted over, eyeing Slocum from top to bottom. A sly smile turned into a sneer.

"You have returned. As a common laborer?" He motioned to the driver of the supply wagon to leave.

"Go on," Slocum told the young man. "Thank Mr. Gutherie for the offer of a job, but I reckon I've got one here. Isn't that so?"

"Of course it is," the maharajah said, grinning even more broadly. The sneer had turned into an evil leer. "You will scout for me."

"Need a horse," Slocum said.

"Of course you do. Go to the elephant pen and tell Gasim to give you one from my remuda. Choose well. The horse must have stamina enough to keep up if I choose an all-day excursion."

"Like you did today?" Slocum saw the lathered team and welts where Ali had whipped the horses unmercifully.

"You are a man who misses nothing. This is perfect for a scout. You will find me a bear. A grizzly, you called it. I would hunt one to see if it is as ferocious as a tiger." The maharajah made his dismissive hand gesture. "I think not, but it will be an interesting experience, no matter how tame this bear might actually be."

"Whatever you say," Slocum said, swallowing his pride. The prince laughed as he went off to his tent without so much as a backward glance.

By this time Lakshmi's servant had popped out of the rear of the carriage and come around to help her to the ground. Ali drove off, snapping the reins and further abusing the team.

"Enjoy the tour?" Slocum asked Lakshmi.

She appeared surprised that he had spoken to her. She looked at her servant, then in the direction Ali had driven.

"It is not safe to speak to me. He is very possessive."

"The maharajah? What harm is there in exchanging a few civil words? Or is that the problem?"

"What do you mean?" Lakshmi blinked. Her ebony eyes drew Slocum in like a whirlpool sucks in unsuspecting sailors. Her nut-brown skin gleamed with a thin sheen of sweat from the hot afternoon sun, which made her about the loveliest woman he had seen in months. Darlene was far out of this elegant princess's class.

"From the way he treats folks, common civility is a rare commodity in these parts."

"He is a prince, a ruler of many, many people. He does not have to be polite when he has the power of life and death in his hands."

"So in India he can order a man killed and that's it? Somebody does it?"

Again Lakshmi glanced in the direction of her servant. Slocum got the idea that the man was less her servant than the maharajah's spy. He thrust out his hand.

"My name's Slocum. Pleased to meet you."

Lakshmi's servant recoiled, staring suspiciously at Slocum's outstretched hand. Then he looked from the open hand to Slocum's face.

"I am Valande." The man was short, sturdy and carried a pair of ornately gilded daggers at his belt. A pink scar running from a ruined ear to his jaw marred his otherwise handsome face. "Is this proper?" Valande suddenly asked Lakshmi.

"We are not in India. The customs here are strange," Lakshmi said. "Go, prepare my tent."

Valande hesitated. Again Slocum had the feeling the servant wanted more to hear what Lakshmi might say than to obey her. He finally bowed his head and walked away slowly, his good ear tilted slightly backward in their direction.

"He is a loyal servant," Lakshmi said.

Slocum waited to be sure Valande was out of earshot before he said, "Are you sure?"

"He is a spy," Lakshmi said unexpectedly, "but do not let on. The maharajah would kill him."

Her burst of honesty took Slocum aback. He had anticipated protests of innocence and loyalty.

"What about you? Do you tell the prince everything he wants to hear, too?"

"You are not a foolish man, Mr. Slocum. Do not act churlish." With that, Lakshmi hurried to her tent. Slocum saw the flap of the maharajah's tent move slightly although the faint afternoon breeze had died completely. Either the maharajah himself, or possibly Ali, had been watching from across the common area between the tents.

Slocum hefted his saddle and set off for the elephant pen to find Gasim. It took the better part of ten minutes to get there. He was tuckered out by the time he reached the area. The elephant wallowed in a mud puddle at the far end of its pen. Slocum approached and scratched its head. The knee-high stone fence that formed the pen was so flimsy that the elephant need only kick out to topple it. It wasn't even high enough to prevent Slocum from jumping it. If he could do that, so could an elephant standing fifteen feet tall.

"What do you want?" Gasim appeared like a ghost. Slocum swung around, dropping the saddle to protect his body if the mahout tried to stab or shoot him. Gasim stood with his arms hanging at his side. He might not be friendly but he wasn't going to stab Slocum in the back. Not right now.

"Why does the elephant stay in an enclosure like that?" Slocum pointed to the law rock wall. "Seems like it could jump it and be halfway to Cheyenne by morning."

"Elephants do not jump. They cannot."

"It can't step over that wall?"

"No. I wanted to dig a foot-deep trench. That would serve the same purpose but the ground dirt is like rocks."

"Sun-baked," Slocum said.

"Yes, that is so. It is not like India where the ground is soft from many rains." Gasim looked almost human for a moment as he fondly remembered his native land. The expression vanished quickly. "What do you want?"

"I've hired on as the new scout. The maharajah said you'd let me pick a horse from your corral." Slocum looked around and wondered where the horses were kept. He suspected that elephants and horses were a bad mix to corral together and that decent riding animals might be a distance off.

"You work for the prince now?"

"That's what I said."

"Clean the pen," Gasim said. A smile showed broken teeth. "You must muck the pen."

"Got a shovel?"

"Use your hands."

"That what happened to Hugh Malley? You ordered him to do your work for you and when he refused, you had your elephant stomp on him?"

Gasim took a step forward, hands balling into fists. Slocum estimated the distance and knew the mahout would never be able to land a single punch. Slocum had been in too many bar fights to let anyone have the first blow.

"You refuse? You miserable cur?"

Slocum tossed his saddle directly at the mahout. Gasim was a wily fighter and knew better than to try to catch the gear, but he still staggered as he sidestepped the flying saddle. Slocum swarmed in behind and let fly with a straight jab that connected and knocked Gasim to the ground. The mahout sat there, looking more startled than hurt. Slocum figured no one had ever decked him before.

Slocum gestured for the mahout to get up so they could continue the fight.

"Gasim!" The name snapped with all the authority of a whip being cracked.

Slocum glanced over his shoulder and saw the maharajah sauntering up, Ali close behind. The maharajah's servant held his hand near a sheathed dagger at his belt. If he touched the hilt Slocum was going to throw down on him. A bullet always beat a thrown knife.

The maharajah rattled off a sharp string of commands in Hindi that caused Gasim to bow his head. He got his knees under him but remained in a kneeling position so he could touch his forehead to the ground.

Slocum decided Gasim was no further threat, but he watched Ali closely.

"If that's what you expect from all your hired hands, reckon I'll be moving on," Slocum said. He glanced from Gasim to Ali.

"He should not have been so impudent," the maharajah said. "He will be punished. Please stay, Mr. Slocum. I am in need of a good scout."

Slocum saw that Ali left his hand so that his thumb hooked under his belt, near the hilt of his knife. Slocum faced off against the servant, turning his side to the prince.

"You might need me but I can't say I feel the same for the rest of your men."

The maharajah said something in a tone equally as sharp as he had used to address Gasim. Ali crossed his arms over his chest and glowered.

"He is overly protective of me. When he saw how you had manhandled Gasim, Ali thought you were a threat to me."

"No threat, if I get my horse and I don't have to muck the elephant's stall."

The maharajah's eyes widened, then he laughed.

"You do not have to clean up after this noble creature or the other en route from Cheyenne."

"You've got another of those beasts coming?"

The maharajah's eyes locked with Slocum's.

"The young one on its way here is a special elephant. A baby, hardly more than eight feet tall. But a special one. A white elephant."

"Royal elephant," muttered Gasim, never lifting his eyes.

"Yes, a royal elephant."

"A white elephant?" Slocum wondered about that. He had seen snow hares with perfectly white fur. Other creatures that didn't hibernate and had to eke out an existence in the snow also turned white in season, but elephants were creatures from jungles. Hot jungles.

He thought the maharajah was pulling his leg.

"Mr. Slocum, go find yourself a horse in my corral." The maharajah smiled his superior smile. "I am sure you will find one that pleases you." The maharajah made his dismissive gesture to hurry Slocum on his way to the remuda on the far side of camp, then began berating both Ali and Gasim in his native tongue. Slocum quickly left the trio behind to find the corral.

Slocum chose a white stallion.

8

Slocum found life in the camp mostly boring. The maharajah's servants tended the prince constantly, administering to his every whim. What Slocum couldn't figure out was Lakshmi's position in the pecking order. She rode with the maharajah often and he treated her differently, although not too politely. Lakshmi might have been a wife, but Slocum got the feeling she was more of a mistress or concubine. Valande was her servant but the man spent as much time elsewhere as at her beck and call, often leaving her alone in her tent.

Seeing that Lakshmi was by herself so often emboldened Slocum. He thought he might find out the truth of Hugh's death from her more easily than from any of the servants. Getting the maharajah to admit that he was responsible for either killing Hugh or ordering him killed was a pipe dream. Whatever evidence there might be, Slocum had to unearth it by himself—or with Lakshmi's help.

He finished currying his horse and returned it to the corral on the south side of the camp, as far from the elephant pen on the north as possible. Slocum found the servants tight-lipped and almost fearful of him. That might be from whatever Ali or Gasim had said about him, but Slocum got the distinct impression that horses and elephants did not mix well. He considered asking the mahout directly but wanted nothing to do with Gasim, if possible.

Even thinking of the mahout made Slocum's spine tingle. He vowed to never turn his back on Gasim and that wicked dagger he carried at his belt. He added Ali to the list of men to never trust, if there was even a hint that the maharajah's opinion of his scout changed.

Slocum looked around the camp and saw only a few servants scurrying on errands that he knew nothing about. Valande was gone, and Lakshmi was alone. Slocum edged closer to the woman's tent. If she was something less than a wife, she might be willing to help him. Slocum had to admit some mistresses were more loyal to their men than wives, but he had seen the way Lakshmi looked at the maharajah and the high-and-mighty way he treated her.

She would help him find out what had really happened to Hugh Malley.

Slocum veered away from Lakshmi's tent when Ali came out of the maharajah's quarters and stood, arms crossed on his broad chest. He glared at Slocum, who politely touched the brim of his hat and kept walking. Out of the servant's sight, Slocum cursed his bad luck. Another few seconds and he could have slipped in to talk with Lakshmi. But Slocum decided his luck might have changed when he saw Valande hurrying out of camp, looking around furtively.

Slocum made sure that Ali remained at his post outside the prince's tent before following Valande. Lakshmi's servant looked too sneaky not to be up to something he shouldn't be doing. Hanging back, Slocum knew he would have no trouble finding Valande's tracks in the grass and soft dirt. Crushed grass stalks took an hour or more to pop back. Lakshmi's servant was only a minute or two ahead.

Taking his time, Slocum trailed Valande into the foothills

a mile away from the camp. Something warned Slocum to approach cautiously as he neared a particular tumble of rock. This place hadn't been selected solely because it was well away from camp. There had to be something more— and he reckoned it was because anyone hidden in the rocks could watch the approach.

Slocum crouched in tall grass and waited patiently. He had lost sight of Valande long since, but his caution paid off. A flash of sunlight off metal high in the rocks showed him where a sentry watched the trail to the meeting spot. Moving slowly to prevent the grass from betraying him, Slocum edged along until he reached a barren stretch below the rock where he had seen the reflection.

From here it was a matter of speed mixed with a healthy dollop of quiet. Slocum swarmed up the rock, barely disturbing a lizard sunning itself. Otherwise, no guard would have heard his approach.

". . . not so," came the voice floating on the still air. Slocum wiggled forward on his belly to see Valande and Gasim. From the way they stood almost nose to nose, Gasim was Valande's superior and was berating him for some infraction.

The conversation, if it had ever been in English, turned back to Hindi. All Slocum had to go on was the way the two men stood and the tone of their voices. Valande had done something woefully wrong and was getting chewed out for it.

This added to his knowledge of who was in charge in the maharajah's camp. The Indian prince was at the top of the heap, but Gasim was further up the ladder than Lakshmi's servant. From the terse replies Valande made, he had little to report and this did not set well with Gasim.

Slocum slipped back knowing he wasn't going to learn anything eavesdropping. Ali might outrank Gasim, but not by much. Ali's power probably came from being the maharajah's personal servant rather than his elephant driver.

Deciding not to try to beat the two servants back to camp, Slocum found a comfortable niche in the rock and waited. Ten minutes later Valande hurried away, shoulders slumping and his stride that of a defeated man. Less than five minutes after he had vanished into the tall grass on his way back to camp, Gasim followed. His head was held high and, although Slocum could not see his face, he was confident in his stride.

Long after Gasim disappeared, heading for the elephant pen, Slocum sat and thought as he sucked on a long blade of grass. He could not see that the maharajah had much to do with Hugh's death but Gasim had to know what had happened. If anyone controlled the huge beast well enough to get it to trample a man, it was Gasim. And Valande might be a part of the plot.

For two cents, Slocum would have strung up the entire lot of them, but he had to be sure he missed nothing. He wanted to know what had happened and who was responsible for Hugh Malley's crushing murder.

Knowing that he would be missed in camp if he lingered too long, Slocum slid from his cranny in the rocks and returned to camp by a route that made it appear he had been off on the prairie rather than up in the rocks. Men who met secretly like Valande and Gasim had to be up to something suspicious. It took less than twenty minutes to reach the spot where he had pitched his camp and sink down to think a bit more on what he had seen.

"Mr. Slocum, are you ready for a hunt?"

Slocum straightened from pretending to clean his gear to see the maharajah, resplendent in a black velvet jacket chased with gold threads in curious patterns. Behind him stood Ali, a heavy rifle held in the crook of his arm.

"What are we hunting? More buffalo?"

"I have bagged enough of those shaggy beasts. While there is some thrill, hunting Cape buffalo is more challenging."

"What's a Cape buffalo?" asked Slocum.

The maharajah laughed his superior laugh and said, "A large black monster that roams southern Africa. It is quite sporting to kill one."

"Only used one shot," Ali chimed in.

The maharajah made his chopping hand motion to silence his servant, but Slocum saw the man was secretly pleased that his marksmanship was noted and appreciated.

"We shall hunt for these wild cats you call pumas or cougars."

"Mountain lion," said Slocum. "They go by a lot of different names."

"We shall see if they are a match for the tiger."

"You going to take along a big company?" asked Slocum. "Cougars turn wary if they hear a lot of men coming."

"No beaters?" Ali seemed disappointed.

"Mr. Slocum is the expert on these wild beasts. Very well," the prince said, slapping his thigh as he came to a decision. "Get Gasim. We shall hunt from the back of the elephant."

Slocum started to point out that a handful of men could spook a mountain lion enough to send it running for the timberline. An elephant would chase any self-respecting mountain lion into the next county. As fierce as the cougars could be, they avoided humans through long and painful experience. In earlier days when only mountain men prowled the slopes of the Grand Tetons the cats might have been more prone to attack, but they had learned when more and more men came to settle the land that avoidance was better than attack. Eat one small child and packs of hunters pursued until the killer cat was run to ground, gunned down and skinned.

"They're scarce critters," Slocum said. "We might not spot one the first day."

"Then we prepare for many days. However long it takes.

Tell Gasim," ordered the maharajah. Ali bowed slightly, took a step backward and then turned to leave.

"You will not shoot, Mr. Slocum. Only I will hunt this mountain lion. It is to be mine and mine alone."

Slocum nodded. He had no quarrel with any mountain lion in these parts. From the abundance of game he had seen, any cat was likely to be fat and sassy but probably not stupid. It might be necessary to track one to its lair.

"Let the hunt begin!" The maharajah whistled as Gasim brought the lumbering elephant to a spot a few yards distant, then forced it to kneel so the prince could mount and settle himself into the small box on the animal's back. Slocum took a few minutes to saddle his powerful white stallion and almost five to catch up with the maharajah.

Slocum saw that the elephant's stride was long, powerful and ate the distance like a simple repast. If he was going to scout, he had to remain in front of the elephant. He trotted alongside and called up to the prince.

"There's a canyon a few miles ahead. I'll scout the left branch since it leads higher into the mountains. You might wait at the junction until I see if I've found anything."

The maharajah called down something Slocum didn't catch over the steady clopping of the elephant's hooves and the rattle of his own horse's shoes against a rocky patch. He figured it didn't matter, waved and galloped ahead.

Less than ten minutes later, he slowed to a walk and enjoyed the country the best he could. It was lovely this time of year, but then Slocum found the mountains to be endlessly fascinating in any season. He rode to the junction of the intersecting canyons and cut left. Ahead stretched a U-shaped valley with plenty of hilly sections on either side to accommodate a small pride of mountain lions. He remembered this country from an earlier trip through the Grand Tetons and focused his attention on one spot in particular near a stream where four game trails ended.

Slocum hobbled his horse a hundred yards away, then

sat in the crook of a tree to watch and wait. Deer came
along with a few smaller animals but it wasn't until an hour
before sundown that the cougar silently padded up to the
stream and sniffed about for dinner. Other animals had left
some time earlier. The cat drank its fill, then slipped into
afternoon shadows on the far side of the stream.

Slocum had found his quarry.

He jumped from his tree limb and worked the hobbles
off his stallion, mounted and headed back to fetch the maharajah. Slocum hadn't gone a half-mile when he spotted
the tall, lumbering elephant coming toward him. At first
Slocum thought something was wrong. Then he saw the
maharajah leaning out, his rifle swinging this way and that
as he hunted for his cougar.

Gasim used a hooked pole to prod and his knees to steer
the huge elephant up the middle of the valley while Ali
rode a prancing horse some distance behind, as if to make
sure no one sneaked up on the maharajah.

Slocum watched in disgust as the elephant came up.

"Why didn't you wait where I told you? You could have
frightened off the cougar," Slocum said.

"I am a maharajah. I do not wait," said the prince, glar-
ing at Slocum. "Have you found the prey?"

"There's a stream about a mile in that direction,"
Slocum said, jerking his thumb over his shoulder. "Wait!
Don't go charging there. The cougar left, heading deeper
into the valley."

The maharajah craned his neck as he studied the lay of
the land in that direction. From his vantage, he could probably see a couple miles farther than Slocum.

"There is a trail ahead. A game trail, but it leads into the
hills to the left."

Slocum hadn't known that but was unwilling to let the
prince know.

"That's why they call them mountain lions," he said.
"You might have to go after the cat on foot."

"That's no fit way for a prince to hunt," Ali said. The swarthy man glowered at Slocum.

"This puma is not as ferocious as a tiger," the maharajah said. "I will ride up here. There is more skill required shooting from the *howdah* on the back of an elephant."

Slocum didn't see that as very sporting but kept his peace. He wheeled his horse about and trotted off up the valley, angling toward the left wall to find the trail the maharajah had spotted from elephant-back. Here and there the mountain lion had stepped onto muddy ground and left a big paw print. Slocum had gotten a look at the cat but hadn't realized it was this large. From the size of the paw, it might be eight feet long.

"This way," Slocum called. He knew such loud voices would spook the cougar and send it along its way. Hunting any animal for the thrill of simply killing it wasn't something Slocum cottoned to much. Eat it, fine. Shoot it to keep it from killing livestock, fine. There wasn't any point in stuffing it or putting its head on a wall. If you needed its hide to keep warm, fine. There were any number of reasons to kill an animal, but the maharajah's desire to bag something he hadn't already killed wasn't too high on Slocum's list.

Let the cougar get away. Some rancher might regret this later in the winter when the cat went after a lamb or calf, but that was someone else's trouble.

The elephant lumbered past as the prince spotted his quarry and leaned far to one side of the box to get a good shot. Slocum and Ali jockeyed to get to the side so they could catch sight of the cougar.

"Watch out!" Slocum's warning came too late. The elephant passed by a rock. A tawny flash showed itself suddenly as the cougar pounced. Talons flashed and its powerful jaws opened to clamp fierce teeth on the elephant's side. The teeth failed to penetrate but the mountain lion slid down, leaving behind bloody tracks from its claws.

The elephant trumpeted in pain and shook all over. Slocum saw Gasim fighting to keep his seat, but the way the elephant tossed its head about made it impossible to remain in control. The mahout went flying through the air. But the real problem came as the elephant fought to swing about and defend itself against the cougar. Short tusks of yellowed ivory raked at the cougar and caused the cat to dance away.

All this jerking about loosened the strap holding the maharajah's box. Slocum saw it begin to tilt precariously. Then the prince went flying as the elephant trumpeted its attack and charged forward. The cougar snarled, pawed at the huge, angry, wounded beast and then raced off into the woods where the elephant wasn't likely to follow.

Slocum sat astride his nervous horse, staring at the carnage.

Then things got even more confused. The wounded elephant tossed its massive head, bellowed in triumph at chasing away its enemy and trotted off, back into the valley.

"I'll take care of the maharajah," Slocum shouted to Ali. "Stop that elephant."

To his surprise, the servant obeyed without question. Slocum jumped to the ground and ran to the prince's side. The man lay in a pile of torn jacket and ripped, baggy trousers that soaked up the blood leaking from a nasty gash on his leg.

"I am well," the maharajah said, rolling over. He winced and pressed his hand into his leg. "A wound." As if marveling at such a condition, he lifted his hand and stared at his own blood. "I am wounded in battle with a savage mountain lion!"

Slocum was so angry he could spit.

"Press a cloth against that cut and you'll survive," he

said. Slocum looked around for the mahout but didn't see Gasim. "I'll find your elephant driver."

"Ah, Gasim, yes, go fetch him. He must be punished for causing such a calamity."

Slocum stalked off, then slowed and eyed the ground suspiciously. Cougar tracks. He looked around. The mountain lion that had attacked the elephant had run into the woods a hundred yards away. Then he stared at the ground in front of him. Definite cougar tracks, but these paw prints were smaller.

"Two cats," he cried. Slocum whipped out his six-shooter and ran forward, shouting at the top of his lungs. He saw where Gasim had been thrown down a rocky incline to come to rest at an awkward angle. Gnawing on one arm was a smaller mountain lion—the female he had seen drinking at the stream.

Slocum fired in the air and forced the mountain lion to back away, growling deep in its throat. Gasim's blood dripped from its jowls. The cat let out a feral growl, then bolted into rocks farther down the hill, leaving behind its supper.

"Gasim," came the maharajah's deriding voice. "You made one mistake too many. You fool, you stupid fool."

Slocum's grip on his Colt Navy tightened as he considered shooting the maharajah where he stood. All that stopped him was Ali returning with the elephant.

9

"Your Highness!"

Slocum turned to see Ali returning with the elephant. The maharajah immediately went to stand in front of the wounded animal. Slocum thought that was about the dumbest thing he had ever seen since the powerful elephant could trample the man and never notice.

Like it had Hugh Malley.

"We must go immediately. It's too dangerous for you to remain here," said Ali.

"Nonsense. I have hunted tigers. This mountain lion has its charm."

Slocum looked at the bloody marks on the elephant's side and wondered where the appeal was for the Indian potentate. An animal this large wasn't in danger of dying, but the mountain lion's dirty claws might infect the bleeding wounds—or even cause the elephant to go berserk with pain. That would give the maharajah a real hunt. He could shoot his own elephant.

"Return to camp, sir," Ali said. Slocum saw true concern in the man's dark eyes.

"You do not order me, Ali," the prince said coldly. "I will return to the camp because it is what I must do." The maharajah looked at his dirtied, torn clothing and the gash on his leg that still bled sluggishly. "I need Lakshmi to tend my injuries."

"At once, Highness!"

"I'll ride your horse," the maharajah decided. "Tend the elephant since Mr. Slocum is not likely to be capable of such, uh, wrangling they call it."

Slocum sensed an oblique insult but the prince was right. He could tend a herd of cattle, stop a stampede, do things with horses that the Indian prince could only dream of, but getting a wounded elephant back to its pen was not a chore he wanted.

Slocum and the maharajah mounted as Ali began pushing and shouting at the elephant to get it moving. He had to trot when the beast decided to set the pace just a tad faster than a man could walk, but Ali made no complaint.

"I must bag a mountain lion," the maharajah told Slocum as they rode side by side. "It is a wily adversary, more than I expected from any creature on the North American continent. I am pleased."

"You're pleased?" Slocum shook his head. "You lost your elephant driver and got banged up and you're pleased?"

"Gasim!" cried the maharajah. "I forgot about him when Ali brought the elephant. We must not leave him where he fell." The prince jerked on the reins and turned his horse to return.

"You need to get your leg bandaged," Slocum said. "I'll fetch the body."

"He is my servant. I will do what is necessary to see that his body is not defiled."

Slocum looked at the man and wondered what the hell that meant. He wasn't going to violate the corpse and resented the implication that he would.

"He must be tended properly and the body returned to India," the maharajah said, seeing Slocum's anger. "Religious ritual must be performed to ease his soul on its journey."

"The Celestials render the flesh off the body and send bones back to China," Slocum said. That had never made much sense to him, either, but shipping bones was a better choice than getting an entire body ready for a month-long trip to India. Slocum was more inclined to bury the dead where they fell.

"The Chinese," the maharajah said with distaste. "They covet my land of Rajasthan and will invade someday. How can we stop those faceless, numberless hordes?"

Slocum was more worried about retrieving Gasim's body than some potential invasion of a land he couldn't even locate on a map. Two mountain lions still prowled the area and one had a taste for human flesh. It took close to ten minutes to reach the top of the incline where Gasim had been thrown by the rampaging elephant. Slocum drew rein and frowned as he studied the rocky slope.

"I don't know where the body is," Slocum said. "This is the spot where he took a tumble." Slocum pointed to the cut-up ground, dislodged rocks and even some flecks of blood on rocks a few feet down the slope. Whether the blood came from Gasim or the elephant, Slocum didn't know. But this was the spot where the mahout had fallen.

Now Gasim's body was gone.

"The mountain lion might have dragged off the body," Slocum said.

"Then we track it and save what portion of the body that we can," the maharajah said.

"I'll do it. You don't have a rifle."

"I'll take yours. You have your sidearm."

Slocum bristled at the notion of the prince using his Winchester, but it made sense. Slocum knew the man was an expert marksman after seeing how he bagged one buffalo after another during the stampede. Two guns were certainly better than one when it came to a bringing down

man-eating cougars, but it still didn't set well with him. He
pulled the rifle from the saddle scabbard and passed it to
the maharajah.

"A light rifle, hardly worth carrying," the maharajah
said as he examined the Winchester. "Good enough for
rabbits, perhaps, but nothing more demanding."

Slocum dismounted and made his way downhill without
answering. That rifle had saved his life more than once. It
wasn't a Sharps .50 or the heavy caliber rifle the maharajah favored for hunting, but it could bring down a deer—or
a man.

Slipping and sliding on the loose gravel, Slocum
reached the spot where the cougar had savaged Gasim.
Blood had spattered everywhere. But farther downhill
Slocum saw something that made him cautious. He drew
his six-shooter and looked around, every sense alert for
trouble.

"The mountain lion?" called the maharajah. "Do you
see it?"

"Quiet," Slocum said. "Gasim wasn't dragged off by the
cougar. His body was taken by Indians."

"Of course it was. *We* are Indians," the maharajah said
sarcastically.

"Crow," Slocum said. "He was taken by Crow Indians,
and I don't think he's dead. There's too much blood. Dead
men don't bleed."

"I shall join you." Before Slocum could wave back the
prince, he crashed and slid noisily to stand beside Slocum.
His dark eyes worked over the land and he slowly nodded.
"You are right."

"Thanks for the vote of confidence," Slocum said dryly.
He had already spotted the tracks leading away down a
draw, which took a sharp bend and hid anything in its gravelly bottom. The Crow might be laying in ambush a dozen
yards off.

"Why do you call these natives 'Crow'? When those

who captured Gasim might be other tribes? Is there something in these tracks that identifies them?"

Slocum cursed under his breath since he didn't want to yammer endlessly.

"I ran into Crow hunters earlier. I assume these tracks were made by them or others in their party."

"But you do not know."

"Quiet," Slocum snapped. He cocked his head to one side and listened hard. The wind had picked up a little and whispered through distant leaves, making it hard for him to pick out the sounds mingled with those he needed to decipher most. Turning slowly, Slocum could hear the faint conversation.

"There," Slocum said softly. "The Crow are over there."

"How is it you know they are Crow?" The maharajah refused to let the matter drop. It didn't matter which Indians had taken Gasim. The result would be the same. The maharajah's elephant driver would end up with his scalp lifted if they were hostile. Even if they weren't, the Indians might mistreat the wounded man enough to kill him. Slocum doubted they had seen anyone with that exact skin color, even Mexicans coming this far north to trade. That curiosity might be enough to keep Gasim alive a bit longer.

"Follow close behind," Slocum said. "I doubt they have sentries out, but splitting up will double our chance of being spotted."

"What is happening?" The maharajah tipped his head to one side as he finally heard what Slocum already had. "Are they performing strange heathen rites?"

"They want his scalp for their belts," Slocum said, not wanting any talk at all as he approached the camp. Walking quickly and silently, he went directly along the bank of the arroyo until he got to the wooded area where he heard distinct voices.

Slocum was within a dozen paces of the copse when shadows broke off from two trunks and stepped into the fading afternoon light. He looked down the barrels of two leveled rifles in the capable hands of Crow warriors.

One let out a shrill whistle and brought four other braves running. Slocum put up his hands so they wouldn't shoot.

"I would speak with your chief," Slocum said. His Crow was spotty at best so he stuck with English. The men obviously understood because they whispered among themselves.

"Come." The nearest brave motioned for Slocum to head toward their campsite. Slocum glanced over his shoulder but didn't see the maharajah. He heaved a sigh of relief. There was no telling what kind of trouble the prince might get them into. Slocum's best chance of getting out with his own scalp—and Gasim still alive—lay in palavering with the party's leader. The brave might not be a chief but Slocum knew he had to treat him as such.

He stepped into the clearing where two small fires sputtered. The evening meal was yet to be prepared because the Crows were too interested in their captive. Gasim was tied to a nearby pine tree, his hands behind him. His eyelids fluttered, and he hardly recognized Slocum. But he was alive.

Slocum hoped they'd all be able to brag about that when morning came.

"I greet the great chief of the Crows," Slocum said, holding out his hand. A brave beside him made a grab for his six-shooter, but Slocum moved too fast, sidestepping so the man missed.

"Kill him," spoke a young buck. He looked like a stripling compared to some of the others, but his voice carried the sharp edge of command that set him apart. He might not be a chief—yet—but there was no question that he was in charge of what looked to be a hunting party.

"Does a chief give such careless orders? I thought better of the Crow and their leaders." Slocum took a calculated risk and spat into the fire. His spittle sizzled and a thin column of steam rose.

The Crow shot to his feet, his hand flashing to a knife sheathed at his side. Slocum couldn't help noticing that the jeweled hilt was identical to the one on Gasim's blade. The Indians had already begun divvying up their prisoner's belongings.

"You mock me!"

"Yes," Slocum said. "I thought I spoke to a great chief with wisdom. Am I wrong?"

"No," the brave said, scowling.

"What will you trade for your prisoner?" Slocum indicated Gasim. For the first time since coming into camp, he thought they might get out wearing their hair. Then Gasim's eyes went wide and he struggled, but he wasn't looking at Slocum.

A quick glance over his shoulder confirmed the worst. Slocum saw the maharajah strut into camp as if he owned it. He didn't even have the Winchester leveled at the Crow braves but carried it over his shoulder like a soldier on parade.

Gasim rattled off a long burst of Hindi, but the maharajah ignored his servant as he came to a spot a few paces away from where Slocum stood by the fire.

"Primitives, the lot of them," the maharajah said.

"Primitives who'll scalp you if you get them mad," said Slocum. "And maybe they'll scalp you even if you don't piss them off."

The Crows stared at the prince, one even coming close enough to run his fingers over the maharajah's fancy velvet jacket. The threads caught the firelight and turned to liquid gold. That first touch was tentative, almost fearful, but the next was bolder. Soon, all the Crows were running their hands over the jacket.

"A mighty chief like you should have a coat like that," Slocum said to the young buck leading the hunting party.

"It is yours. A gift from another mighty chief."

The maharajah looked a bit surprised.

"Give him your coat," Slocum said. "Don't argue."

Slocum had to give the prince his due. The man was quick enough to understand the situation so that he shucked out of the jacket and even held it for the Crow brave to slip into. To Slocum's surprise, the jacket might have been tailored for the Crow. It fit perfectly.

"A fine gift to show friendship between our people."

"His skin and his," said the Indian, rudely pointing to Gasim and then to the maharajah, "are the same. Not like the white man's flesh."

"I am from a far-off land," the maharajah said. Slocum shook his head slightly. He didn't want the prince mucking up the exchange. It had gone well so far. The Crow turned around and around, fascinated by the way the light reflected off the golden threads in the jacket.

"He would take his brother back to this far-off land," Slocum said. "We will trade for the one you have tied up."

"Pants," the Crow said suddenly. "I want." He pointed to the maharajah's baggy trousers.

Slocum was afraid this would be a problem, but the maharajah agilely shucked off the pants and handed them to the brave, adding a small bow that was not lost on any of the Crows. They hooted and hollered and looked on top of the world. Slocum hoped they weren't also interested in taking the maharajah's silk underwear.

"You are a mighty chief and mighty chiefs keep their word. Release your prisoner," Slocum said. The brave made a gesture identical to that used so familiarly by the maharajah. Two braves hurried to Gasim's side and cut the ropes holding his hands. Slocum was pleased to see that the mahout had enough strength to get to his feet and unsteadily walk over to them. To support him now would jinx the deal.

"Come to our camp," Slocum said graciously since he

wasn't giving away anything that belonged to him, "and we will give you many more gifts, gifts worthy of a great Crow chief."

Slocum silenced the maharajah with a look, but the man seemed pleased at the notion of the Crows coming to his camp.

The Crow nodded once, then crossed his arms over his chest. Slocum saw how the brave's fingers continued to stroke over the intricate patterns formed by the threads on the jacket. Gasim struggled to walk but the mahout left the Crow camp on his own. When they reached the spot where Slocum and the maharajah had left their horses, Gasim reached the limits of his strength and collapsed.

"Put him on your horse," the maharajah said in his usual imperious tone. "He cannot walk in this condition."

"He's lost a lot of blood," Slocum said. A quick examination showed Gasim's wounds were clotted over but serious enough to require him to stay in bed for a week or more. Even then, his injuries might not heal properly since the mountain lion had ripped away part of the muscles in his upper arm.

The maharajah had already ridden off, head high in spite of his semiclothed state. Slocum settled Gasim and then mounted, steadying the man. The powerful stallion hardly noticed the extra weight as they trotted to catch up. Slocum would have joshed anyone else about returning to camp in only baggy underwear but decided the maharajah was not the joking type.

They reached the camp around midnight. To Slocum's surprise everyone was still awake, probably alert for the return of their master. Lakshmi's eyes went wide when she saw Gasim, then she quickly averted her face when the prince dismounted. They exchanged quick bursts of Hindi, but the woman never looked at the partially clad man, as if it was forbidden. Slocum began to wonder what the relationship was between Lakshmi and the maharajah. If they were married, seeing him in such dishabille wouldn't be that unusual.

Lakshmi bowed deeply and backed away from the maharajah. Ali held open the tent flap for his master, then vanished inside after him.

"I need some help with Gasim," called Slocum. To his surprise, Lakshmi hurried over. She did not seem uncomfortable at the sight of so much dried blood.

"He is nearly dead," she said, as if accusing Slocum of being responsible for Gasim's condition.

"We got him away from a party of Crow hunters. They took a fancy to him because of the color of his skin. They might be Indians, but they don't see folks from India in these parts."

"This wound is from an animal bite." Lakshmi's fingers expertly probed Gasim's shoulder and biceps.

"A mountain lion mauled him. Are you a nurse?"

"I am trained in many disciplines," Lakshmi said. She looked at him and those impenetrable ebony eyes took on a spark of fire, just for a moment. Or was Slocum reading something that wasn't there? She hurriedly summoned servants and ordered them to take Gasim to a tent.

Lakshmi turned to Slocum and started to speak when the maharajah returned, fully dressed once more.

"You have performed a great service, Mr. Slocum. While you lost us the mountain lion, you saved our favorite mahout. Take this as a token of our thanks." The prince held out a small box.

Slocum took it and opened the lid. For a moment he was not sure what he was looking at. Lakshmi gasped and muttered under her breath, "Such a fine diamond!"

"Thanks," Slocum said. "I'm glad that Gasim is getting the medical help he needs."

He stared at the large rock inside the box as the maharajah left, trailing Ali and Lakshmi. He had seen diamonds before but never one the size of a large pebble. It had to be worth a fortune. Slocum looked around but he stood alone in the middle of the maharajah's camp, as if everyone else had simply evaporated. He tucked the box into his pocket and tugged on his stallion's reins, getting it moving toward where he had pitched his camp. He might not be any closer to figuring out who killed Hugh Malley but he was a sight richer, thanks to the maharajah's reward for saving Gasim.

10

With the huge diamond rubbing against his chest as it bounced around in his shirt pocket as he rode, Slocum headed into Hoback Junction to see Darlene. The constant reminder of the diamond told him he was rich when he sold it—and that he wasn't likely to figure out what killed Hugh Malley if he got the money and rode on. Had the fancy diamond been a bribe so Slocum would do just that? The miner was dead and was hardly more than a faint memory in the maharajah's camp. If the prince had ordered Hugh's murder, it was unlikely Slocum could get any of the servants to fess up. It was even less likely he could get Gasim or Ali to speak of his friend's death.

Slocum laughed ruefully. The one most likely to confess was the elephant, and Slocum didn't speak the animal's language. Not like he did horses, He patted the neck of the powerful white stallion the maharajah had given him and sobered a mite. Was he willing to forget Hugh and how he had died because the prince had bought him off? Slocum touched the diamond and wondered if that hunk of gemstone meant as much to him as getting this fine horse.

The maharajah was a clever man and obviously knew everyone's price. Slocum hardened at the thought of being bribed and not even knowing it. Resolve grew until he came to a decision. He wasn't going to give up on finding who had killed Hugh and why. It might have been that Hugh had seen something people in the camp wanted to keep secret. That would be a good road for Slocum to begin traveling once he returned from town.

The day was hot and only a feeble breeze blew across the Wyoming prairie, but the Grand Tetons rising to his back reassured him. He was in the middle of hills and only saw the grasslands because of the direction he rode. Given a few more days, he would solve the mystery of who killed Hugh and why, then be on his way to the upper slopes of the mountains where it was cool and peaceful and there wasn't nary an elephant to be heard trumpeting.

Hoback Junction seemed particularly empty for midday, but Slocum paid scant attention as he looked around for a jeweler's store. The closest he came was next door to the land and assay office. A big sign outside listed all the items of precious metal that would be purchased "for a fair price" inside. Diamonds weren't listed, but Slocum had confidence that he could get enough money for the rock to keep him from sleeping in the stables.

He went into the shop and looked around. His nose wrinkled at the pungent stench of spilled chemicals. The chemist, decked out in a heavy canvas apron and thick gutta-percha gloves, looked up.

"What kin I do fer ya?" He didn't sound too eager to leave his experiment. A bluish liquid in a clear Mason jar awaited a twisted hunk of metal the man held in clamps just above the surface.

"Go on, finish whatever you're doing. I'm in no particular hurry," Slocum said. The chemist grumbled, then dropped the bit of metal into the blue acid.

"Aqua regia," the chemist said. "Dissolves damn near anything. Got me a good silver ore sample here. But you don't wanna hear that, do ya?"

"What can you give me for this?" Slocum drew out the diamond in its box and lifted the lid to expose it to the faint light slanting through the solitary window in the shop.

"I declare," the chemist said, picking up the diamond and peering at it closely. "This real?"

"Reckon so," Slocum said.

"You got it from that India fella, din't ya?" The chemist took the stone to the dirty window and dragged it across the surface with a screech that put Slocum's teeth on edge. A shiny cut in the glass testified to the diamond's authenticity, not that Slocum had doubted for a moment that the maharajah would give him a worthless hunk of glass.

"What'll you give me for it?"

"Ten," the chemist said, dropping it on the counter.

"Ten thousand?" Slocum's eyes widened.

"Ten dollars. I ain't got no market fer that thing. Nuthin' I kin do to break it up into smaller hunks, though I heard tell of diamond cutters doin' that."

"Ten dollars?" Slocum was getting angry. "It's worth more than that!"

"Not to me, not to nobody in Hoback Junction. You want top dollar fer it, you take it to New Orleans or maybe St. Louis. Don't think you could get more 'n five hundred for it in Frisco, 'less it caught the eye of one of them high-priced whores." The chemist chuckled at a private joke. Slocum asked what was so funny. "Well," said the chemist, "I was thinkin' you could give that to the best lookin' whore in all of Frisco and get yerself laid for the next twenny years. I'll give you fifty for it!"

Slocum tucked the diamond back into its box and left without another word. He hadn't expected this. If the man had offered a few hundred, Slocum would have been inclined to accept, but fifty dollars was a tiny fraction of what it was worth. As he walked, his ire settled. The chemist was right. Who in Hoback Junction, Wyoming, wanted such a fabulous precious stone? Most of the women, the ones who had any jewelry at all, wore rhine-stones and were happy for that speck of flash.

The diamond might be worth more than the land under the entire town but did him no good if he couldn't find anyone interested in buying it.

Slocum went to the hotel and asked after Darlene, only to find that she had taken a clerking job at the general store. He went to the store and looked around. It was empty.

"Hello? Anybody around?" he called. From the back of the store he heard movement and went to see. A young boy, hardly thirteen, played like a cat with a mouse he had trapped in a cracker box.

"Where is everyone?" asked Slocum. The boy jumped like he had been stuck with a pin.

"Sorry, mister. Didn't hear you come in. My pa left me in charge since he and the rest have ridden out to take care of things."

"What are you talking about?" Slocum had the feeling he wouldn't like what he heard. Hoback Junction seemed unnaturally empty right now.

"They got themselves a posse together and went out to string up all them Indians. Well, they ain't Indians like we know. Those brown-skinned fellows what killed Hugh Malley."

"Darlene," Slocum muttered.

"Yep, she convinced my pa and a dozen others around town. She rode with 'em. She's not all that good-lookin', but she rides like a man. And I heard her cussin'. She can cuss a blue streak, too."

"I bet she can," Slocum said. "When did they leave?" He hadn't passed them on the road as he came into town.

"Oh, they left 'fore dawn. They was gonna split up and go at the Indian camp from a couple different ways so none of them varmints could get away. They was a little a'feared of that elephant. Don't much blame 'em, but I'd sure like to see it 'fore they kill it."

Slocum doubted the maharajah would care much if the posse shot all his servants, but if they touched one bristly hair on the elephant's back, he would use that rifle of his to take out the men one by one. With such a large caliber rifle, he could shoot them from horseback at a half mile and never even need to squint.

"There's supposed to be another of them elephants comin' to town."

"What's that? Another elephant?" Slocum remembered something the maharajah had said about this.

"Bein' brung in from Cheyenne, or so I heard," the boy said. "Cain't say why since they don't look to be good for much, other 'n scarin' the little kids." He obviously did not place himself in this group.

Slocum left the general store without another word. Darlene had whipped the townspeople into a blood frenzy that would end up in too many more deaths. She wasn't content letting him poke about and wanted revenge for Hugh herself.

As Slocum galloped from town he saw Marshal Rothbottom leaning against the jamb of the door leading into his jailhouse. The peace officer glared at Slocum but said nothing. Slocum wondered if Rothbottom knew half his town was out ready to string up anyone with strange clothes and smelling of elephants or if he was completely oblivious to what went on around him. It didn't matter since the outcome was the same either way.

Someone was going to die, and it wasn't necessarily the one responsible for Hugh Malley's death.

As he rode at such a quick pace, even the powerful horse began to tire. Slocum changed gait, then had to stop for a spell to let the horse cool off and regain its breath. Slocum was in a hurry to get to the camp to warn the maharajah, but only because *he* wanted to be the one who found who had killed Hugh Malley. Slocum knew a lynch mob such as the one Darlene had gathered would care nothing for truth or justice. They'd be whipped into a murderous frenzy and whomever they came across would be the victim—guilty or not.

As he brought the horse into a walk, Slocum saw dust from off to his left. The spectacle of the Grand Tetons was dwarfed, however, when he saw that the approaching rider was the lovely Lakshmi. Her long black hair flowed behind her, caught on the wind like some delicate banner. Expensive clothing glinted in the sunlight and the occasional jewel on her person added to the belief that a drop of sun had come to earth to shed its brilliance. To his surprise, Lakshmi was an expert horsewoman and flowed well with the animal straining so under her.

"Mr. Slocum!" she called. "Please. Help. We need your help."

"Whoa, slow down," he said as she jerked back on the reins. Her horse dug its heels into the ground and sent up a dusty curtain all around. By the time she had settled down, they were almost leg-to-leg but facing in opposite directions. This gave Slocum a perfect look at her finely chiseled features, the darkly beguiling eyes and the strange red dot painted on her forehead.

"Ali, they have Ali. They caught him some distance from camp. They were sneaking about. I happened to see them and told the maharajah. He told me to ride to town and get the marshal."

Slocum snorted in contempt at the idea Marshal Rothbottom would do anything to help. In a way, Slocum was surprised that the peace officer wasn't with the crowd, helping them knot the hangman's noose.

"Where is he? Not in camp?"

"I avoided the road to ride here, but no, you are right. Ali is several miles toward the foothills. The maharajah must have sent him on a hunt for berries or—oh, I do not know! I saw them shoving him back and forth. His hands were tied. A woman wanted the men to 'string him up,' she said."

"Darlene," Slocum muttered. Louder he asked, "How long ago was that?"

"Not more than ten minutes. Even with my detour off the road, not more than that."

"Dismount. Give me your horse," Slocum said, thinking fast. "I can't gallop mine long enough to get there since I've already tuckered him out, but your horse is still fresh."

"Very well," Lakshmi said, unsure of what was happening. She dismounted. Slocum jumped from saddle to saddle. The spirited mare Lakshmi had ridden tried to show him who was boss, but he quickly settled the mare's nerves.

"Go back to camp, but if it looks like the posse's coming, hide out until they're gone."

"All right," Lakshmi said, but it was to Slocum's back. He bent low over the mare's neck and used spurs and reins to urge the horse to full gallop. The mare wasn't as strong as the stallion but had not been ridden into the ground already.

The distance flew past and then seemed to drag when Slocum picked up tiny sounds ahead. The noises became more distinct, and then he heard men crying out angrily for blood. It hadn't taken long for the posse to become a lynch mob, and they were going to string up Ali for the hell of it.

The mare faltered and almost fell but recovered and kept on galloping gamely until Slocum reached a tall oak with a thick limb. The first thing he saw was the hangman's noose dangling over the branch, swinging slowly in the sluggish Wyoming wind.

A dozen yards away the posse had gathered in a circle and shoved a bound Ali back and forth to get him dizzy and disoriented. Darlene sat astride her horse, watching with a fixed expression that sent shivers up Slocum's spine. He had seen men with tombstones in their eyes before but never a woman so intent on a man's death.

"Who was it?" she demanded. "Who murdered Hugh? Tell us and we'll let you go."

"You will kill us all," Ali cried. For his impudence, a man swung his rifle and caught the Indian on the back of the head. Ali stumbled forward and fell to his knees. The men began kicking him until he stood again. His back was straight and his chin held high in defiance. They could kill him, but they'd never get him to implicate anyone in Hugh's death.

"He's not going to say a word. String him up," Darlene said, as cold as Judge Parker sending another man to the gallows.

"Wait a minute," Slocum shouted. "Are you sure he's the one who murdered Hugh Malley?"

"What's the difference?" Darlene asked. Slocum ignored her. She incited the crowd to violence, but he had to throw water on their fiery tempers if he wanted to save Ali. Worst of all, he didn't actually *want* to save the Indian servant. Letting him swing at the end of a rope was probably too good for him, but his death wouldn't answer the real question of how Hugh had died.

Or why he had died.

"You want the real killer. String this one up and you might get him, but you might let the actual killer go scot-free," said Slocum.

"Then we gotta introduce 'em all to a good ole-fashioned Western necktie party!" shouted someone in the crowd.

"Hang the innocent with the guilty? How'd you like it if Marshal Rothbottom worked like that back in Hoback Junction? He might take it into his head to arrest the lot of you for stringing up the wrong Indian."

"They look alike," another in the crowd said. "You sure," he called to Darlene, "that this varmint's the right one?"

"She doesn't know who killed Hugh any more than you

do—than I do," Slocum said. He saw some weaker sisters in the crowd wavering. He kept talking and finally drove a wedge through their resolve. Slocum caught his breath and held it when he saw the maharajah riding up. The prince carried one of his powerful hunting rifles. There was no telling where he had been. He probably had waited some distance off, ready to shoot anyone trying to actually hang Ali. Seeing Slocum easing the lynch mob away from their murderous ways, he chose to show himself.

Slocum wasn't sure that was a good thing, especially if the maharajah acted uppity like he had a yen to do.

"Good afternoon," the maharajah greeted, as if he had simply come upon fellow travelers along a road. "Out for a constitutional?"

"What's that mean?" asked a ruddy-faced man.

"For your health, sir. Are you British, by any chance?" The maharajah's question confused the man. Slocum had to admit he wasn't alone. What was the prince up to?

"Me a Brit? Hell, no. I hail from down around New Braunfels, just outside of San Antonio in Texas."

"German?"

"Reckon so. Leastways, my pappy was so that makes me half German. My ma was a mestizo from down in Mexico, but we're all Texans through and through."

Slocum didn't interrupt. The peculiar questioning went on as the maharajah went from man to man asking if they were of British descent. By the time he had finished, the posse had lost all sense of purpose. Nothing Darlene could do stirred them to the same need for blood that had brought them from town.

"Take your manservant, Maharajah," Slocum said. "See that he's tended."

"Quite," the prince said, eyeing Slocum. The maharajah grabbed Ali by the collar and pulled him over the hindquarters of his horse, hands still tied behind him. When he rode back toward his camp, the spirit left the lynch mob entirely. They drifted away by ones and twos until only a fuming Darlene was left.

"We could have got the truth from him. He would have told who was responsible for Hugh bein' tramped on like he was."

"This isn't the way to find whoever's guilty," Slocum said. "I told you I'd find out, and I meant it. Get on back to town. Let me keep poking around. They don't trust me enough to talk, but I'm finding out plenty."

"Such as?" Darlene glowered.

"I'll let you know when I can tell you for sure who murdered Hugh," he said.

"You better or I swear, John, I swear you'll be swingin' from one of them oak tree limbs!"

Darlene rode off, madder than a wet hen. But Ali hadn't gotten his neck stretched.

Slocum mopped sweat from his forehead, then turned the mare back toward the road and Lakshmi. This was his first and best chance to talk to the woman and find out what she knew of Hugh's death—and the strange questions the maharajah had asked of the crowd.

11

Slocum found Lakshmi standing beside his horse along the road. He wondered if Darlene and the rest of her lynch mob had ridden past, but he doubted it from the anxious expression on the Indian woman's face. She knew nothing of the outcome and would have known immediately if Darlene had come this way.

"Is everything all right?" Lakshmi asked anxiously.

Slocum dismounted and handed her the reins to her horse. He had used the mare as lavishly as he had his own stallion. Both horses were lathered from heavy, hard riding and deserved to be cleaned, curried and fed in addition to getting a good, long rest. Slocum found himself smiling a little at the idea that he deserved the same.

"Ali almost got his neck stretched," Slocum said. From her puzzled look, Lakshmi had no idea what that meant. Slocum explained.

"The barbarians!" exclaimed Lakshmi. "They would murder an innocent man!"

Slocum didn't share the exotic woman's appraisal of Ali—or anyone else in the maharajah's camp. Hugh Malley had been murdered, and it was passed off as an accident with no investigation of the circumstances at all.

"We should rest the horses," Slocum said, looking around. "Over yonder." Slocum pointed to a meandering stream some distance from the road. The grassy area on either bank would give the horses something to nibble, and a few low-growing stunted trees afforded a bit of shade.

"I must return to the camp."

"Ali's fine," Slocum said. "The maharajah showed up after the crowd had decided to go home. He took Ali back."

"They are not hurt?"

"Nope," Slocum said. He was already walking his stallion to the stream. Lakshmi could do as she saw fit, but his expert eye caught signs that her horse would not go far before collapsing. Lakshmi had ridden it hard from the maharajah's camp, and Slocum had given it an even more strenuous run.

"You are right," Lakshmi said, a smile dancing on her lips. She brushed back her midnight-dark hair and lifted her chin slightly to let the gentle breeze caress her face. She closed her eyes and let out a small, contented noise like a kitten purring. Slocum studied every plane of her beautiful face, her lush body, the tempting way the wind pressed her elaborate dress against her body and then released it, taunting him.

Lakshmi opened her eyes and stared straight at Slocum. He caught his breath. He worried that she might not like the intent way he studied her, her body, everything about her. If anything, she welcomed it.

"Come," she said, reaching out and taking his hand. Together they walked to the stream. "We should rest along with our horses."

"Reckon so," Slocum said. The way she looked at him told him they wouldn't be doing much resting. He quickly unsaddled the horses, hobbled them so they could crop at the knee-high grass and drink from the stream and not wander away. As he turned back, he stopped.

Slocum stared.

"Sorry," he said, not sorry at all. Lakshmi sat under a gnarled oak tree entirely naked. She had shucked off her dress and anything she had worn under it. Her mahogany skin shone in the light filtering through the gently dancing leaves, casting tempting shadows here and there as the wind picked up a little.

Lakshmi had breasts the size of large apples and twice as tempting. Her waist was narrow and her hips wide. She sat with legs drawn up slightly to occasionally reveal the dimly seen, furred patch between her thighs. She reached out. Long fingers rippled as if she had no bones in them as she beckoned him toward her.

"Are you sure about this?" he asked.

"You Americans are so formal at the wrong times," Lakshmi said. "What is it about me that you do not want? Do I not have fine breasts?" She cupped her teats and lifted, then pinched the already hard nubs capping each. She sucked in her breath as she gave herself a jolt of pleasure. "Or can it be my belly is too fat?"

Lakshmi lounged back slightly as she ran her long fingers across her firm, flat stomach. Those fingers pointed lower. She saw Slocum's attention—and how he responded.

"Perhaps you do not think this region is desirable? Too tangled? Not lush enough?" Her fingers stroked over her privates even as she moved her legs to alternately give Slocum a bold view and then a more chaste position with her legs drawn up tightly.

"Or do you think I am inexperienced? I know the *Kama Sutra* well. From personal exploration, not merely academic study."

"What's that?" Slocum dropped his gun belt and was kicking off his boots when Lakshmi laughed.

"I should show you. The *Kama Sutra* is not to be talked of. It is to be exalted by action. Intimate action."

"I've got to agree. I'm in favor of doing rather than talking, too," Slocum said. He dropped his shirt and began working off his jeans. He was aware of how Lakshmi stared at him with rising desire. Her fingers no longer strayed to other parts of her body but remained hidden between her legs. Her hand moved up and down, and Slocum knew what she was doing—what he wanted to be doing.

He watched her closely as her hand stroked up and down and her arousal mounted second by second. Slocum responded to the sight by getting harder. He stepped closer and looked down at her. He felt a tremor pass from head to toe at the beautiful sight before him. The sleek nut-colored skin, the hair and breasts and legs—it was all enough to get any red-blooded man excited.

Slocum knelt and gently parted her legs to expose her nether regions. One of her fingers curled around and disappeared inside that moist, tight recess.

"Let me put something else there. Something we'll both enjoy a whale of a lot more."

"No!"

Her sharp refusal startled him. He could not have read her wrong. She was the one who had stripped off her clothing to entice him. And her arousal was obvious. The brown nub on each teat was hard and pulsing with need, begging for his lips and tongue and attention. Her chest heaved up and down as her heart raced. Why did she tell him "no"?

"We must proceed slowly if I am to show you one page of the *Kama Sutra*."

"What's that mean?"

"It is the Hindu book of love," she said. Her tongue slipped out and made a quick circuit of her lips. She fixed her dark ebony eyes on his green ones. Then she reached out, and he knew she wasn't turning him down. She wanted to show him how Indians made love. He was so throbbingly hard that he would have hung upside down from a tree limb if that opened her book of love to the right page.

He jerked when her fingers lightly brushed along the

sensitive underside of his erect organ. She tapped and stroked, then pinched. The difference in sensations took him by surprise. Slocum fought to keep control.

"You see, there are many ways of stimulation," she said softly. Lakshmi moved closer so her hot breath gusted into his ear. A wet, darting tongue touched his lobe and tried to stuff itself into his ear before moving on. Lakshmi kissed and touched with her tongue to leave a wet spot before blowing on it. Cool, hot, neutral, aroused, she guided him through all possible sensations.

He tried to kiss her but Lakshmi drew back.

"Let me do for you," she said softly as she rubbed her breasts against his naked chest. He felt the hammering of her heart. She seemed cool as a cucumber, but he felt the heat from her radiating into his body. Slowness in her movement masked her desires.

"Build slowly," Lakshmi said. Her mouth moved fleetingly across his. Her tongue stroked his and then found a new target.

"This is fine, but I'm getting mighty excited," Slocum said. "Have been getting more excited from the first day I set eyes on you. You're about the prettiest woman I've seen in a month of Sundays."

"The prettiest," Lakshmi said, her breath coming faster now. "And the most skilled. I have watched your soiled doves as they made love. They know nothing."

"You've what?" Slocum thought he was past being flabbergasted by anything anyone could say or do. He was wrong. "How do you know what goes on between a whore and her customer?"

"The maharajah has sampled their wares," Lakshmi said, continuing her oral assault. She added the lightly dancing fingertips to her stimulation of every inch of Slocum's body.

"And you watched? Did he know?"

"Of course. He ordered it. I was not distressed at the request. I desired it. In India, lovemaking is an art. Here, it is more like a rodeo."

"Yeehaw!" cried Slocum. This brought a laugh to the woman's lips.

"You are so different," she said. "I must show you much so you will be pleased with me."

Slocum tried to answer and found the words all jumbled in his throat. Her hands had both dropped down to his manhood. Lakshmi moved her hands up and down, in concert and in different directions. Whatever she did excited him that much more. Slocum was harder and hotter than he remembered ever being.

"I should do something for you," he said.

"You are. Can you not tell?" Lakshmi shoved her chest forward again and he felt her heart hammering away.

"I want to do more."

"You will. Oh, you will!"

With her gentle urging Slocum sat cross-legged on the ground so she could straddle his waist. Slocum gulped as he felt the sensitive underside of his manhood rub against the crinkly nest between Lakshmi's legs. She circled his waist with her legs and tensed, pulling her body in closer so she sat on top of his thighs, their privates working slowly as her body undulated. She was dancing to a tune Slocum didn't share. He was eager to enter, but she restrained him.

Just as he was sure he could not hold back another instant, she pressed and pushed and moved in such a way that it was possible. Every time, he found himself brought to a higher level of excitement, barely restraining himself—but succeeding.

He lifted a bit off the ground, but she silently pushed him back down using only the pressure of her hips. She wrapped her arms around his neck and began kissing.

Slocum thought he knew everything there was about kissing, but he quickly learned there was more. And Lakshmi showed him. Not only did she kiss but also her roving fingers sometimes intruded.

Slocum found himself sucking on her fingertips and then her tongue, only to have delicious sweet-wine lips against his. She engaged him perfectly as she ran those knowing fingers down his spine, outlining every bone and sometimes pressing in forcefully.

Every time she did something new, he jerked and thought he would lose control. But he didn't and found himself aching for her more than he ever had for another woman. Still she wouldn't give him the release he sought.

Lakshmi began moving her hips in slow, subtle circles. First she rotated clockwise and then reversed her course. Her body rubbed into the underside of his manhood and promised paradise—but never quite delivered. This teasing caused him to reach a new plateau of arousal.

"I want—" That was as far as he got. Lakshmi's hips rose and she moved still closer. This time, however, as she descended she enveloped him entirely.

"Now," she whispered hotly in his ear. "Do for me what I have done for you. Make me yearn for what only you can give me."

As much as Slocum wanted to lift her up, flop her onto her back and sate himself, he realized she was offering him far more than a sudden physical release. She was offering him the sexual experience of a lifetime.

He could not duplicate the delicate motions of her fingers. Besides, he did not know the right spots to press and stroke that would send the electric volts of delight into her body. His callused fingers did their best to stroke and stimulate. He ran his hands down her sides, traced out ribs, then slipped across her lower back, cupped her firm buttocks with his strong fingers and began to knead as if he had found two mounds of tasty brown dough. Buried within her, he found a different way of exciting both himself and her as he twisted about in a corkscrewing motion.

Slocum knew she was responding to his ministrations by the way she uttered tiny animal noises. More than this he felt her tensing around his hidden buried length. He gulped and kept going in spite of the tensions reaching the breaking point inside. She massaged him with hidden muscles and then threw her head back, letting her hair fly about wildly. Slocum realized he could not keep going much longer.

He lifted her a little off his lap and then let her settle down slowly. This up and down movement brought even more violent reactions in the supple woman. She jerked about like a whip being snapped and then let out a louder, longer cry of releasing desire. This almost ended Slocum's valiant efforts to keep his control.

She crushed him as desire blasted through her. Slocum kept up the slow movement until Lakshmi reached down and found the hairy bag dangling under his long shaft. As he moved her body up and down, she began massaging it with her fingertips. The feathery touches coupled with the inner heat and moisture leaking out around his thick, fleshy plug set him off. He made no effort to hold back. The sensation ripping through him was too intense for that.

He heard Lakshmi crying out in ecstasy again, as if she were in the distance. The marvel of their lovemaking shook him and unleashed something more than simple physical pleasure. Slocum held Lakshmi close and then slowly disentangled their arms and legs to lie in the grass under the tree. He looked into her lovely face. The woman's eyes were closed and her expression was one of contentment. Eventually, she opened her eyes halfway.

"You have read the *Kama Sutra*, also."

"Never heard of it before today."

"You are a natural talent."

"I had some powerful inspiration," Slocum said. For a spell they said nothing more, content to let the warm Wyoming breeze caress their bodies as they lay still.

It was some time before Slocum asked, "What are you to the maharajah? You're not his wife, are you?" Slocum was startled at the reaction this caused. Lakshmi sat bolt upright, her eyes wide.

"His wife? You joke! We could never marry. That would be a travesty."

"Any man'd be a fool not to have you under him. Or over him or any of those positions you were talking about."

Lakshmi almost smiled, then turned somber.

"I am more than a servant but less than a concubine."

"A mistress?"

"Not that. The prince and I have never . . ." Lakshmi made a vague gesture with her long-fingered hands, indicating what she and Slocum had just done. "It is more complicated than that."

"What do you do for him?"

"I am a secretary and translator, since I speak languages he does not. And anything else he might want done."

Slocum didn't quite understand but let it drop. He had other questions to ask of Lakshmi and felt the moment would slip away like tickling a slippery rainbow trout if he failed to ask now.

"What's the dot? The red spot on your forehead?"

Lakshmi blinked and frowned.

"You jump from one thing to another. But this? This is *bindi*," she said. "It is made of turmeric mixed with other spices. It shows many things. In some regions of Rajasthan only married women wear it. In others, a white spot means unmarried but not available. In my case, it means unmarried but . . . skilled."

Slocum didn't bother asking what skill that might be. He had found out firsthand. As fascinating as it was to hear her murmuring, soft voice and look into her dark eyes, Slocum had other fish to fry.

"What's the maharajah want? He's not just hunting wild creatures to put in his trophy room." Slocum remembered how peculiar the prince had acted afterward when it was obvious that Darlene's lynch mob wasn't going to string up Ali.

"I am not sure. He has not confided this in me, nor has he asked for me to gather information. I do know this: He is most interested in anyone of British citizenship."

"What?"

"He hired your friend because he was British."

"Hugh was Welsh. A coal miner. What earthly use would Indian royalty have of someone who grubbed out a living a mile underground?"

Lakshmi shrugged her bare shoulders, causing a delightful jiggling reaction down lower. Slocum forced himself to ask a couple more questions.

"What do you reckon he wants with a Brit? It's not just any Brit, is it?"

"I think he looks for someone in particular, but as I said, he does not trust me with such information." Lakshmi turned slightly toward him so he got a better view of her lovely breasts. He saw that the nips were hardening again—just as he was down low.

"How many pages are there in your book?" Slocum asked. He reached out and lightly touched her cheek. She turned her head a mite and kissed his palm.

"Many," she said in a low, husky voice. "Many, many pages. We should not dawdle if we are to get through one or two more."

"Only one or two?"

"I do not want you to learn too much," Lakshmi said, kissing his chest and looking up with her limitless dark eyes. "You would have no further need of me."

"Don't be so sure," Slocum said. "And don't think

everything's in that book of yours. I might be able to show you a trick or two."

"Do it!" Lakshmi said eagerly.

Slocum did.

12

Slocum worried about Darlene back in Hoback Junction and the trouble she might be getting into. He didn't want to ride along, always watching his back trail and worrying that a lynch mob was going to swoop down on the maharajah or Ali or any of the others in the Indian camp. Slocum wanted to find out the details of Hugh's death and work from that base. Somebody had done his friend in, and Slocum was going to find out who.

Then the guilty party would pay. With his life.

Slocum and Lakshmi had returned to camp after twilight bathed the camp in long shadows and turned the tents into some exotic far-off location. The elephant bellowing in the distance added to the feeling of being transported into another world. Or was he only thinking of his unique lovemaking with Lakshmi? He had never experienced such sensations before and wanted more, like some opium addict.

But Lakshmi had been summoned immediately by the maharajah and had vanished into the prince's tent for more than an hour. Slocum had hung around, studying the camp routine and wondering how the labor was divided among the servants. Most of them were lower caste. Slocum was getting a feel for the differences in class status. Not all of them were treated as slaves. One group could dictate to another, but then bowed deeply when a higher caste came along. The maharajah was at the top of the pecking order, but Slocum couldn't figure where Lakshmi fit in. She was a woman and lower status, or should have been. Yet her caste, whatever it was, allowed her to dictate with almost the same authority as the maharajah.

Almost.

Slocum saw how her servant, Valande, spied on her. Valande and Gasim were in cahoots, with the mahout higher in caste. But why did Lakshmi permit such spying? Slocum scratched his head. She was no fool and had to know she had a traitor in her own employ. The only thing Slocum could decide was that Lakshmi knew and fed bogus information to Valande for her own purposes.

Or was the situation in the maharajah's party entirely beyond his comprehension?

Slocum had watched Valande, Gasim and Ali moving about, watching Lakshmi and the maharajah and one another but never coming together to compare notes. He had finally given up around midnight and unrolled his blanket for a decent night's sleep. The commotion in the camp just before dawn brought him awake. He heard footsteps coming in his direction and reached for his six-shooter, keeping it out of sight under the edge of his blanket.

"The maharajah wants you. We hunt today," said Ali, looking as impassive as if his face had been carved from a block of walnut wood.

"What are we going after?"

Slocum spoke to empty air. Ali was already halfway back to the main area of the camp. Slocum stretched and tucked his six-gun away. His belly grumbled, but he decided it was better to present himself for the day's hunt rather than grabbing a fast breakfast.

He hurriedly pulled on his boots and saddled his stallion before leading it to the maharajah's tent.

Slocum was not surprised to see the man facing east, eyes closed as he waited for the sunrise. As the first rays touched the prince's face, his eyelids opened slowly to take in the full beauty of dawn in Wyoming.

"You are ready, Mr. Slocum?" he asked without turning. Slocum thought the prince was worshiping the sun, but that didn't jibe with what little he knew of the Hindu religion.

"What are we hunting today?"

"Bear. Your stories of these ferocious animals have piqued my curiosity. I have decided that the mountain lions were not such ferocious beasts, after all."

"Clawed up your elephant, and Gasim isn't likely to get full use of his arm back," Slocum pointed out. "That's mighty ferocious in my book. Especially since we never even got a good shot at the puma."

"That the elephant is injured is a shame. I fear we cannot use it until it heals since the wounds have become inflamed."

"Did I hear you say that you're shipping another one from Cheyenne?"

"A special elephant, one more fitting for a maharajah. The large gray elephants are useful but not suitable for truly regal travel. I intend to move on in a few days, when the white elephant arrives."

"Never seen a white elephant," Slocum allowed. "Saw an all-white man once. An albino, they called him. White hair, skin whiter than bleached muslin, though his eyes were pink like a rabbit's."

"You would be disappointed then. The Indian white elephant is not white but dust-colored. Most unusual."

"And fit for royalty to ride," Slocum finished. From the hot flash of anger this inspired, Slocum thought it was better for him to keep quiet.

"Ali will range ahead and beat the bushes today," the

maharajah said, his ire subsiding as Gasim brought a horse for the man to mount. Gasim dropped to hands and knees and let the maharajah use his back as a stool to mount.

Slocum swung into the saddle. He caught sight of Lakshmi peering out of her tent. She smiled and waved almost shyly to him, then ducked back inside. Slocum had to use his spurs to catch up with the maharajah and Ali, both of whom had rocketed from camp and were heading toward the mountains.

"Does Ali know what spoor to look for? You might want me to scout and let him hang back," Slocum suggested.

"Ali is a clever man. He will know," the maharajah said. "I want to have a word with you."

Slocum tensed. In spite of what Lakshmi had said, she might belong to the maharajah in ways other than sexual. The maharajah certainly wouldn't take kindly to Slocum and Lakshmi being together the way they had. Slocum shifted a little in the saddle so he could get to his six-shooter if the need arose. He didn't want to gun down the man, but he had seen how good a marksman the prince was. If he drew the rifle riding at his knee, the maharajah would be a formidable foe.

Slocum didn't want it to come to a shootout between a pistol and a high-powered rifle.

"Do you know any Britishers?"

The question took Slocum by surprise. Of all the things he had expected, this was not it.

"I have since learned that your friend Malley was not British, not technically, but a Welshman. That is most unfortunate."

"His death or that he was Welsh?"

"Why, both, naturally," the maharajah said, his eyebrows rising in twin arches. "You do not think Mr. Malley's death was accidental, do you?"

Since Slocum thought the maharajah might be implicated, he held his tongue.

"I am more interested in finding a British citizen. To your knowledge, are there any in the area?"

"I was just passing through," Slocum said. "There might be some. Usually are, though I know more Irish and Scotch than British."

"No, not Irish. Not Welsh or Scotsman. The man I seek must be from London."

"What's your interest in this gent?"

"Ah, look, Ali is signaling to us. Perhaps he has found bear scat or other sign."

Slocum looked around and nodded. This was the type of country bears preferred. Mountainous, a stream running not far off probably loaded with trout, plenty of fodder growing here and up the side of the mountains where a bear could make a den. Bear country.

Slocum touched the rifle riding in his saddle sheath but knew better than to use it. The prince wanted to make the kill. Besides, Ali might not have found a bear at all. Slocum didn't trust the man's tracking ability all that much. In the jungles of India he might be good, but this was the West.

The maharajah broke open the breech of his rifle and shoved in the heavy cartridge.

"Yes, I do so love the British. I should find one of their number among the throngs out on the Wyoming grasslands."

Slocum looked sharply at the maharajah, wondering if he was being sarcastic. He could not tell from the man's tone, but the words indicated he wanted something more than a pleasant conversation or afternoon tea with any British citizen he found.

"There!"

Slocum sat bolt upright in the saddle. Ali had flushed a bear, and it was a big one.

"Brown bear," Slocum said in a low voice, not wanting to draw any more attention to himself than necessary. "Not a grizzly."

"So it is not worth shooting?" The maharajah lowered his rifle and hesitated as if thinking it over. His horse began backing and threatened to bolt and run as it caught the bear's scent. The prince controlled it with his knees while he brought the rifle to his shoulder again.

"It's coming this way!" Slocum grabbed for his rifle, but the approaching bear caused his stallion to rear and paw at the air. Slocum was off-balance and fell heavily to the ground. He struggled to get to his feet but couldn't get traction on the grassy stretch where he lay sprawled. He rolled, grabbing his rifle as he got out of the bear's path.

The maharajah's horse let out a frightened neigh and finally forced him to grab for the reins. The horse ran away with him, leaving Slocum to face the bear on his own. He kept rolling as he pulled the rifle in close to his body, then he slammed against a rock and came to a sitting position. From this awkward posture he brought the rifle up and squeezed the trigger.

The hammer fell with a dull thud.

Slocum hastily levered another round into the chamber and immediately felt the new cartridge jam in the action. He struggled to clear the breech, but the bear roared and charged straight for him. Ali had been too effective in flushing their quarry.

Slocum dropped the rifle and sprang to his feet. His hand flashed for his six-shooter and whipped it out to fire point-blank at the bear's head. He saw the bear recoil as the .36 caliber bullet smashed into the heavy-boned skull directly between the eyes, but the slug wasn't heavy enough to do any damage to such a powerful beast. Slocum had struck it at the thickest portion of its skull and had only enraged it further.

He tried to scramble up the rocks behind him, but the bear was on him in an instant. Powerful, hairy arms circled him and tried to crush the life from him. Slocum winced as claws cut painfully into his back, holding him in place against the bear's broad, smelly chest.

Slocum had heard stories of how mountain men had escaped such a deadly embrace. No man was strong enough to fight a bear, even a brown bear, but many were brave enough and clever enough to know the habits of such an animal.

Slocum went limp in the bear's grip. He closed his eyes and held his breath, hoping against hope he did not appear alive any longer. Bears ate live food. He had to convince the bear that he was dead. No matter how powerful the shaking, Slocum remained as limp as a dishrag. With a furious roar, the bear threw him a dozen feet. Slocum hit the rock, felt skin being ripped off and let himself slip down. He hoped his acting was good enough to convince the bear he was dead.

The brown bear roared in rage. A loud report sounded and rock chips showered down on Slocum's face. He winced. Opening one eye a fraction he saw that the bear had lost interest in him because the maharajah was firing methodically at it with his powerful rifle.

Roaring as it reared on hind legs, the bear issued its challenge to the maharajah. Then the bear reconsidered its defiance and dropped to all fours. With impressive speed, the bear headed for the thicket a dozen yards away and vanished from sight. Slocum continued to lie doggo, not wanting to risk having the bear come roaring back.

"I say, Mr. Slocum, are you dead?"

Slocum opened his eyes. The maharajah stood over him, the rifle pointing directly at his chest. For a moment, Slocum wondered if the real threat came from this man rather than the bear, but he figured the maharajah could have plugged him at any time.

"I'm scratched up but still in one piece—I think." Slocum winced as he tried to move his left arm. His shirt was soaked with the sluggishly flowing blood from the claw tracks on his back.

"I fear I missed the monster. He was a powerful beast. But you say he was not a grizzly?"

"A brown bear," Slocum said, standing. Every bone in his body ached as he moved, but he was alive. He had always wondered if the tall tales spun by the mountain men were true on how to keep from getting killed by a bear. He wished he could stand all of those rugged men a drink for actually telling the truth.

It had saved his life.

"I must find Ali. Where did he go?" The maharajah rode away, clutching his rifle and looking about for his servant.

Slocum picked up his rifle and examined the action. He went cold inside when he saw how the jammed cartridge had been bent. He pried it loose and saw several scratch marks on the side of the brass. Slocum looked around and found the first round that had misfired. The primer was missing. He had tried to fire a defective shell, then had pumped in a bent cartridge.

Someone had sabotaged his rifle and hoped it would kill him.

It almost had. Now he was fuming mad.

13

The ride back to camp was slow and, for Slocum, both thoughtful and painful. Every move, every bounce, every time he twisted just a little caused pain to lance into his back where the bear had clawed him. But the pain vanished into a dull ache when he considered how someone had tried to kill him. A jammed rifle while bear hunting was not quite a death sentence, but it was damned close. There was no question that someone had tampered with the first round so it would not fire. They knew anyone having a hang fire on one round would hastily lever in a second.

This had been bent in such a way that it jammed the action. By the time Slocum could have cleared it, the bear would have had him for lunch.

"It is a pity we could not track the bear. For such a large creature, it proved very elusive," the maharajah said. "We might have found it had you been in better condition, Mr. Slocum."

"Sorry," Slocum said sarcastically. "I didn't mean to spoil your hunt by getting mauled."

"Oh, do not worry over it. There will be other days, other bears. If this was not the ferocious grizzly of which you spoke, perhaps we can flush one of them. That would provide a fine hunt."

Before Slocum could tell the maharajah what he thought of the idea, he caught sight of a dozen horses tethered outside the camp. He hardly thought it possible that Darlene had assembled another lynch mob, and if she had, would they be so bold as to ride into the main camp? Mobs tended to be cowardly and preyed on solitary men. To tangle with all of the maharajah's servants would be nothing short of a major war.

"What's going on?" demanded the prince from horseback. He looked down his long nose at the men gathered around the largest of the fire pits in the camp.

"That's Marshal Rothbottom," Slocum said in a low voice. "He's the local law."

"I know who it is," the maharajah said testily. Slocum quieted down. He remembered how the lawman had been loath to come out before and reckoned the maharajah had paid him off. By showing up like this, all bets were off because the marshal had enough firepower riding with him to enforce any law.

"Glad to see you, Your Highness," Rothbottom said. The marshal hitched up his gun belt and looked as if he had eaten something that didn't set well with him. He chewed on his lower lip a moment, then squared his shoulders. "We got business here. Law business. A complaint's been lodged 'gainst one of your folks."

"Gasim?" Slocum looked around but did not see the mahout.

"Who? Nope, Slocum, ain't the elephant driver fella," said Rothbottom. "It's that woman yonder."

Both Slocum and the maharajah were speechless when two deputies dragged Lakshmi from her tent.

"Yep, that's the lady what had charges filed 'gainst her."

"What's she charged with?" asked Slocum.

"Attempted murder. Reckon there'll be other charges

since she didn't actually succeed. Disturbin' the peace, most likely, and dischargin' a firearm inside the town limits of Hoback Junction. That'll keep her locked up 'til we kin get this all squared away."

"Who'd she try to kill?" Slocum saw the confusion and outright terror on Lakshmi's face. He guessed that police taking away a suspect in India was the same as a death warrant. She reached out for Slocum—or was it the prince?—and got manacles clamped around her slender wrists. In a flash she was chained and hauled away.

"We can settle this matter. You said the matter was an attempt at murder." The maharajah rode closer to the marshal, but Slocum saw this wasn't going to work. Rothbottom had men coming up behind him with rifles and shotguns to prevent him from being intimidated or bribed. They weren't going to be robbed of a prisoner this time.

The maharajah was oblivious to the signs as he swung down to the ground and smoothed wrinkles from his dusty clothing. With an easy move, he rested the heavy rifle in the crook of his left arm.

"Who was shot at?" Slocum rode closer and dismounted to put himself on the same level as the marshal. He still towered over the man but didn't make the lawman feel as much like a rat trapped in a corner by standing on the ground.

"That friend of yers," Rothbottom said.

"Darlene?" Slocum wasn't too surprised. If she couldn't get a lynch mob to string up one of the maharajah's men for killing Hugh, she would come at the Indians from another direction.

"We gotta git on back to town with our prisoner." Rothbottom pushed Slocum out of the way. Slocum resisted for a second, then stepped away. This wasn't the place to make a fight of it.

"You'll let her have visitors?" asked Slocum.

Rothbottom chewed a bit more on his lip, then nodded briskly.

"Them's the rules. Only one at a time, then only if'n she wants to see ya."

"Wait, you cannot do this. She is under my protection."

"Wrong, Maharajah," said the marshal. "She's under mine now."

Slocum grabbed the maharajah's wrist to keep him from bringing up his hunting rifle and doing something he would regret. He wasn't supreme ruler here and would end up in a cell next to Lakshmi—or worse. The posse was hungering for a fight. If the maharajah started it, they'd feel all the more righteous about the outcome.

Ali growled like a dog. Slocum favored him with a glare, then tightened his grip on the maharajah's wrist.

"Let it be," he said softly. "We'll work this out, but not here, not right now."

"Do not *ever* touch me," the maharajah said angrily. He jerked free, and stalked off to his tent, Ali trailing behind. Several in the posse snickered and made vulgar comments about a man who wore baggy trousers like that, but the marshal had enough common sense to shut them up before trouble started. They might prevail in a fight but not before several of them ended up candidates for the potter's field outside of town.

Slocum watched the maharajah disappear into his tent and the marshal's posse ride off with Lakshmi, heading back to town. Slocum cursed a blue streak at how dumb Darlene could be, then headed for his campsite to tend to his rifle and check the rest of his ammo for tampering. It took him close to an hour to get himself patched up and his horse and rifle tended before he headed into town. He expected to see the maharajah also preparing to see Lakshmi but the prince had gone to his tent in high dudgeon and had not shown his face. That suited Slocum just fine. It was better if he dealt with the marshal to get Lakshmi free since he wasn't as likely to ruffle the lawman's feathers.

Then he'd have to talk to Darlene and settle matters

once and for all. If she kept butting in, he wasn't likely to ever find out what had happened to Hugh Malley.

As Slocum rode into Hoback Junction he saw a definite change in the sleepy town. Men strutted up and down the street, carrying rifles or wearing iron strapped to their hips like gunfighters. None of them looked as if they had any idea how to use those six-shooters but that made them even more dangerous—they thought they did.

"Figured you'd be along sometime soon, Slocum," greeted the marshal as Slocum dismounted beside the jailhouse. He couldn't keep from wincing as pain drilled into his back and arms. "What's wrong with you? You look all chewed up and spit out."

"Tangled with a bear," Slocum said. His other shirt had been ruined, clawed into bloody tatters. The one he wore was his spare, and it had seen better days.

"Yeah, sure," the marshal said, not believing a word of it. "You want to come on in and palaver a spell? She's been askin' for him, but I reckon she'd be happy to see you."

The inside of the jailhouse was hot and dusty, causing Slocum to choke.

"Be glad you don't have to sit round here waitin' fer some lawbreakin' jist so's you kin go breathe some fresh air," Rothbottom said, trying to make a joke.

"What'll it take to bail her out?"

"Can't do that. I'd have a riot on my hands. The citizens of this here town have taken it into their heads to run off that Indian prince fellow. When they found out the boogey-man scarin' 'em all was an elephant, well, mad don't hardly describe it."

Slocum understood that. The townspeople had been worked up over spirits of the dead and strange monsters lurking in the Grand Tetons, maybe spawned in the Yellow-stone geysers, and had discovered an odd, if commonplace reason for the sounds that had scared the bejesus out of them. They were as mad at themselves for being frightened as they were at the maharajah for bringing the elephant into their mountains.

That made them all the more dangerous. Slocum remembered the sight of the men prancing up and down the street with six-guns strapped on their hips when not one in a dozen had worn such deadly hardware a few days earlier.

"It's not right holding Lakshmi without bail. She didn't kill anyone, after all."

"She'd hightail it at the first chance. She don't live here, after all."

Slocum didn't bother pointing out that if Lakshmi turned tail and ran it might be the best for everyone concerned. He looked past the half-open door into the cell area. The calaboose had all of four cells, made from inch-wide strips of iron riveted together into a cage.

"You wanna go on back and talk, Slocum, you kin do it. But don't take too long. Folks might get kinda uneasy if you're too chummy."

Slocum let the marshal take his Colt Navy and pushed past the door. It had hinges that didn't work, even a little. Once in the cellblock he saw they were rusted completely through.

"John!" Lakshmi rushed to the wide strips of iron and tried to reach through but couldn't do it satisfactorily. That didn't stop her from skinning her knuckles touching his hand.

"What did you say to Darlene? Anything?"

"I do not know this woman! She is the one who came to town with you and Hugh Malley, but I do not know her. Why should I threaten to kill her as they say?"

Slocum made small talk, mostly letting Lakshmi vent her frustration as he studied the jail. The cage only went around on four sides. The door was a separate piece, and the back wall with the heavily barred window in it was not protected by the strips. Slocum wondered if a stick of dynamite would blow out the wall and not kill anyone in the small cell. He doubted it.

"I'll talk some sense into her," Slocum said. "If she drops the charges, the marshal has to let you go."

"The people of this town," Lakshmi said, shuddering. "They will not let me go. What have I done to them to deserve this?"

"Who's the Britisher the maharajah is hunting for?" Slocum asked.

"I do not know!" Lakshmi began crying. She buried her face in her palms and shook silently. "Why do you ask that?"

"Might be it has something to do with the way the folks are treating you," Slocum said. "Or not. This might all be Darlene's doing."

Lakshmi looked up and forced herself to be calm.

"I know nothing about Hugh Malley's death. Gasim said it was an accident. I believe him."

"If the maharajah told Gasim to kill Hugh and then lie, saying it was an accident, would Gasim do that?"

"Yes," Lakshmi said in a small voice. "But why would he?"

"Might have something to do with why he's hunting for a Brit," Slocum said. He didn't think the maharajah would have been so disappointed that Hugh was Welsh that he had him killed, but Hugh might have said or done something to spark such an end.

"Slocum, git your ass outta there. Vistin' hours're over," Marshal Rothbottom shouted from the office.

"I'll get you out of here," Slocum said.

Lakshmi said nothing. The expression on her face told him she doubted that he could do anything for her. That made Slocum all the more intent on freeing her from the jail. He slid between door and jamb back into the outer office and retrieved his six-shooter.

"Don't go stirrin' up trouble now, Slocum. You hear?"

"I understand, Marshal," Slocum said, but that was exactly what he intended doing.

He stepped out of the tiny, close jailhouse into the fresh air and felt a wave of relief wash over him. He didn't cotton much to jails at the best of times, and this was hardly a good time. The only bright spot Slocum could see was that it was Lakshmi locked up inside and not him. With any luck, Darlene would talk to him and they could settle this matter in a few minutes.

Slocum went to the hotel and asked after Darlene, but the clerk said she had checked out. He looked into the general store where Darlene had a job clerking and was told she was in a small building out back. Slocum stopped and gathered his wits. The outbuilding was hardly the size of a coffin, but Darlene was getting free rent here while she worked at the store. From the way the storeowner had talked, though, she wouldn't be here much longer unless she got to work fast. There wasn't room for slackers in Hoback Junction.

Knocking on the door, Slocum waited. He heard scraping noises from inside. Right hand on his six-gun, he pushed the door open with his left. Darlene sat on a three-legged stool beside a cot. She dragged her fingernails endlessly over the top of a small table. Darlene looked up with listless eyes.

"Hello, John."

"Are you all right?" he asked. Whatever had happened to her seemed to have unhinged her mind.

"As good as anybody can be who's almost been killed." Darlene's voice rose in pitch until it was downright shrill. "She tried to kill me. The bitch tried to shoot me!"

"You saw her?"

"I, yes, I saw her." Darlene looked away, studying the scratch marks in the table as if she might discern who had killed Hugh there. Slocum heard something more in her words and hesitation.

"You don't rightly know who shot at you, do you?"

"Her. The Indian bitch! She did it. It had to be her."

"Why?"

Before Darlene could answer, an unearthly screech filled the air. Slocum sprang to his feet and dashed outside, looking around. Screams of panic came from the streets. A new sound replaced the screech. Slocum recognized instantly the exultant trumpeting of the maharajah's huge elephant.

Leaving Darlene behind, he dashed into the street and looked toward the jailhouse in time to see Ali pulling Lakshmi into the small box fitted on the elephant's back. The wall of the hoosegow had been pulled out. Slocum guessed the elephant was more versatile than he had imagined. He slipped his six-shooter back into his holster as Ali urged the elephant to a fast trot out of town.

Slocum looked around. No one was to be seen. All the citizens of Hoback Junction had taken cover at the first sign of the elephant. In a way he couldn't blame them.

But he knew the fear would wear off and be replaced by anger soon. Then they would get their ropes and guns and go hunting for elephant—and Lakshmi.

14

Slocum stood in the middle of the street and wondered how long people had to be gone before a town became a ghost town. Hoback Junction was well on the way if it meant nobody was wandering the streets, no curtains pulled back for fearful looks from the safety of houses, and the law had abandoned the town. Ali, astride the elephant, had spooked the citizens something fierce. Slocum heard movement and turned to see Darlene stumbling out into the street from the mercantile, looking confused. Slocum went to her.

"Are you all right?" Darlene spoke as if someone else put the words in her mouth. "I don't want you hurt, John. You're all I have left. Hugh's dead. And everyone else?" Darlene looked around, as Slocum had been doing. Her tear-filled eyes did no better finding the people of Hoback Junction than his sharper ones had.

"They'll come out of their holes eventually," Slocum said. He put his arm around Darlene's shoulders and steered her to a rickety wood chair on the boardwalk in front of the general store. He gently pushed her down into the chair and knelt in front of her.

"What am I supposed to do, John?" she asked.

"Tell me what happened last night. When someone shot at you."

"I was going to my room behind the store." Darlene pointed vaguely in the direction of the rear of the store. "It was quite dark. I heard a strange sound, very soft, rustling. Like silk rubbing against more silk. Then I saw light reflecting off a gun. I screamed and she fired. That horrid woman. The one you call Lakshmi."

"So you saw her face?"

"Well, no," Darlene admitted. "It had to be her, though. Who else wears silk around here?"

"The men in the maharajah's camp do," Slocum said, remembering the maharajah's own silk trousers. The servants even had jackets made of silk. It was a tough material, light and cool for traveling in tropical climes. For an American, silk was a luxury item. For the Indians it was a useful material, and one the maharajah certainly could afford for himself and those in his employ.

"They do?"

"Could it have been a man who shot at you?"

"The wrist," Darlene said, thinking harder now. "It was a bit thick for a woman's wrist. But I don't know. It might have been, but I think it was Lakshmi."

"Do you want it to be the woman?" Slocum saw the way Darlene's cheeks flushed as she looked away guiltily. She had some idea what might have gone on between Slocum and the seductive, exotic woman. Darlene had lost one sweetheart and obviously had her sights set on Slocum. He wasn't the kind who could be corralled and branded by any woman, and jealousy was only going to get people killed.

Slocum didn't want one of them to be Lakshmi.

"I want them to all leave," Darlene blurted. "Please, John, find who killed Hugh and why. I need to know why they'd do such a horrible thing."

Slocum worried that it might have been an accident, but his gut told him there was more boiling under the surface calm at the maharajah's camp than met the eye. But whatever was there, he doubted Lakshmi would try to kill Darlene. There was no reason he could think of for the Indian woman to do such a thing.

"I'll find out what happened to him," Slocum said. "You keep to yourself and don't go raising any posses." He tried to make it sound light and upbeat but wasn't sure how well he succeeded.

Slocum left Darlene and found his horse. By now a few of the townspeople poked out of their hidey-holes but nowhere did he see Marshal Rothbottom. The lawman might be hiding in the back cell of his jail, if it hadn't been completely destroyed when Ali got the elephant to free Lakshmi. More likely, the marshal was halfway to the next county.

Swinging into the saddle, Slocum trotted from Hoback Junction and headed directly for the maharajah's camp. He needed more information than he had to find out what was going on. He shook his head remembering how innocently this had started. The people in town had heard strange noises, and Hugh had gone after the reward. He had been trampled to death soon after.

Slocum had almost reached the Indian prince's camp when he heard Lakshmi calling his name. He drew rein and looked around but did not see the woman.

"Here, John, over here." Lakshmi stepped out from beside a tree alongside the road. Her expression was tense. Slocum knew she had reason to be worried, not knowing when the marshal would get his posse together to come after her for breaking out of jail.

"You've certainly stirred the pot a mite since the last time I saw you," he said. "Why'd you break out of jail? I told you I'd talk to Darlene. She admitted to me that it might have been a man who shot at her. All she saw was a hand holding a gun. She thought it must be you because she heard the sound of silk sliding against silk."

•

"But all the men wear silk clothing," Lakshmi said, dismayed.

"She would have dropped charges," Slocum said. "Now you've got to dodge the marshal for jailbreak."

"I did not want to leave. I was going to do what you said, but Ali came with the elephant." Lakshmi looked even more distressed.

"We can smooth it out, but you're going to have to pay for the damage to the jailhouse," Slocum said.

"Please, that can wait. I have found something, John. I was going through my brother's papers and—"

"Your brother?" Slocum was confused. Lakshmi looked at him. Her thin eyebrows rose and the red *bindi* dot between her eyes seemed to crinkle with the beginnings of real humor. For the first time Lakshmi smiled broadly, even if she did not laugh outright.

"My brother," she said. "I thought you knew. The maharajah is my brother."

"I didn't even guess," Slocum said.

"He is not a maharajah, either. He is only a raja. Still important but lesser in rank. Our father might one day be maharajah, but I do not believe it will happen."

"That's all?" Slocum asked. "Your brother's not really the high muckety-muck he's been pretending to be?"

"No, no, John. He is quite an important man, but he puts on airs when he is abroad. Please," she said in exasperation. "I found why he came to your West. He is looking for a British citizen, a remittance man."

Slocum frowned. Many British lords had second and third sons who would never inherit either title or family estates because of the law of primogeniture. Rather than keep a useless drone about, these sons were often shipped off to America where they received a small allowance every month to stay away from the serious business of running the family estates. Most of these remittance men were drunkards and ne'er-do-wells Slocum viewed with the same contempt he did any wastrel unwilling to work for a living.

"Why does he want to find this Brit?"

"I do not know. All I saw was the paper with the man's name. Will Harrison. From maps he lives somewhere on the eastern slope of the Grand Tetons."

"That sure cuts down on where to look for him," Slocum said sarcastically. There must be a hundred thousand square miles of rock on the eastern slope of the mountains.

"I have a specific location." Lakshmi held out a map. Slocum took it and spent a few seconds getting oriented. He turned slowly, matched the map with topographical features of the Grand Tetons and then quickly figured distances.

"Might be a day's ride off. Two at the most. What is this place where Will Harrison is?"

Lakshmi shrugged her lovely shoulders.

"If we find Harrison, what's in it for us?" asked Slocum. "Will your brother fess up to what happened to Hugh Malley?"

"I do not know," Lakshmi said, "but I do know that he will leave Wyoming and America when he finds Will Harrison. I want to leave, John. Please do not take this wrongly. I hate this place. I hate all that has happened, and I miss my own country. In this country no one can tell another's social caste and everything is so wild and confused. I wish my brother had never brought me along."

"You didn't have a choice?"

"He is my brother," she said, casting her eyes downward. "In my country women do not have the freedom they do in yours."

Slocum snorted. Wyoming was different from most other places in the country. From what he had heard, they agitated to give women the vote and even had mentioned the possibility of a woman being governor. But folks in Wyoming were considered strange everywhere else he traveled throughout the West, even—especially—in adjoining Utah Territory.

"I'm not traipsing off to find this Harrison fellow unless I get answers to how Hugh died."

"Please, John, for me. I must leave this place."

"Take that up with your raja brother."

"I . . . I cannot. The reason I rifled through his papers was because of Ali."

"What's he got to do with this?"

"He is not the loyal servant my brother thinks. Ali tried to imprison me."

"But he rescued you from jail!"

"He tried to bind me and hide me in the mountains. He intended to barter me for Will Harrison."

"What's Ali's interest in this remittance man?" Slocum read the answer on her face before she could answer. Lakshmi didn't know. All she knew was the name and location of the man her brother sought.

Apparently Harrison was important enough for Ali to risk royal displeasure by kidnapping a princess and ransoming her for the man. Or maybe what Harrison knew. This was mining country. Maybe Will Harrison had found a rich mine and the maharajah was somehow involved in ownership.

Slocum shook his head. It felt as if it might break apart it ached so. None of that made sense. The only way to find the truth was to find Will Harrison.

"Let's go," Slocum said.

"What are you saying, John?" Lakshmi's eyebrows arched again.

"I can't leave you behind. Ali would catch you. And if he couldn't, he might decide to kill your brother if he thought you had told him anything. Does the maharajah even know you've been busted out of jail?"

Lakshmi shook her head and looked miserable.

"Then we're going to find Harrison and get to the bottom of this. Do you have a horse?"

"No, I escaped on foot. What am I to do?" Lakshmi sounded almost panicked.

"I'll steal a horse. Then we'll go see Harrison ourselves. You stay out of sight."

Slocum was taken aback when Lakshmi threw her arms around his neck and kissed him hard on the lips. He felt her body melting to match the contours of his. Worse, he began to respond to her passionate kiss. Slocum pushed her away.

"I'll be back as fast as I can."

Lakshmi caught her breath, then let it out in a sudden gust. She dropped her eyes and nodded.

Slocum slipped into the maharajah's camp and got a horse with gear without anyone seeing him. He returned to Lakshmi and they were on the trail heading deeper into the Grand Tetons within a half hour.

15

"Were there other papers in your brother's files?" asked Slocum. It was hard for him to get around the words and the notion that Lakshmi was the maharajah's sister. "Something else he could use to find Will Harrison?" Slocum worried that the maharajah's henchmen would take out after Lakshmi and figure reaching Will Harrison first was the best way to capture her again. From everything he had seen at the camp, the servants always jumped when the maharajah gave an order, but such instant obedience could cause hatred of their master. Slocum didn't know what would have turned Ali against the maharajah but it had to be something potent that had built over the years.

Slocum sucked on his gums a moment, reflecting. Lakshmi might have gotten confused. It was possible that the maharajah had ordered Ali to break his sister out of the Hoback Junction calaboose and then keep her safely out of sight until they finished their hunt for Will Harrison. She might have interpreted that as being kidnapped by Ali working on his own. There was too much he didn't know and even more that he simply guessed at.

Lakshmi did not answer right away. Slocum looked at

her as she took a sharp bend in the trail. She might not have heard him since she looked to be as deep in thought as he was. He had a powerful lot of facts to sort through, not the least being her relationship to the maharajah. A female maharajah—whatever that'd be called—obviously had less power than royalty in other countries. Slocum had heard that Great Britain, at one time a couple hundred years back, had a queen on the throne. That might have been unusual, but Lakshmi showed no hint that she held any power other than the servants scuttling around her brother's camp. Her own servant spied on her and looked to be in cahoots with Gasim.

All the servants were in league against her, Slocum decided, since Ali had broken her out of jail only to try to get the information out of the maharajah where Will Harrison was. The pot was definitely coming to a boil.

He caught up with Lakshmi. She looked at him and smiled weakly.

"You are a savior, John. I do not think I could have found Harrison without you."

"We haven't got him yet," Slocum pointed out. "Why didn't your brother plow right on up into the mountains and find him on his own? The map isn't that hard to figure out."

"I do not know," she said. "He was spending a great deal of time hunting. He is a great hunter and has bagged many tigers in India, but his heart was not in it. He was waiting, but I do not know why."

"Did he suspect his own servants might have wanted Will Harrison for their own purposes?"

"I don't know. I know so little. I just want to go home."

Lakshmi's shoulders sagged as she rode. Slocum wondered what was going on between her and her brother. Why had he brought her to America at all? There was too much he didn't know, but at least he had the map Lakshmi had stolen from the maharajah's tent. Slocum held it up and matched it to the mountains ahead. The beauty of the

Grand Tetons vanished as he studied the canyons and peaks, the location of lakes and rivers.

The distance to the mountains was deceptive because of the clear air. On the plains he often felt as if he rode in a fog, unable to see more than a mile or two at a time. But here in the mountains, he could look down and out and see for miles and miles. It made Slocum a little heartsick thinking that Hugh Malley would never see this. Then he smiled ruefully. Hugh Malley would not have appreciated these vistas. He had been a hard-rock miner whose idea of a good view was a new vein of ore a mile underground.

"Let's break for something to eat," Slocum said. They had been on the trail for better than four hours, putting a considerable number of miles behind them. It was time to let the horses rest.

"There's a good spot," Slocum said.

"I want to keep going, John," Lakshmi said. "The sooner we find this Harrison the sooner I can go home."

"And leave me behind?" Slocum's tone was light, but Lakshmi acted as if he had stabbed her.

"I am so sorry, John. I did not mean it like that."

Slocum waved off the apology. He jumped to the ground and hobbled his horse so it could eat without wandering off. At last he got a chance to look around without having to struggle with the map while on horseback. Something about the lay of the land bothered him, and he couldn't put his finger on what it might be. They were at the juncture of three valleys, one going deeper into the Grand Tetons, the one they had just traveled and another coming in at an angle.

"What's wrong?" Lakshmi asked.

"The other canyon. That one," Slocum said. "I wish I had a map showing where it led."

"Back toward Hoback Junction, I should say."

"You're probably right. That might be the canyon where Hugh Malley was supposed to go scouting for the weird noises in the night." As Slocum spoke, he thought of Hugh and how long ago it seemed that they had driven into Hoback Junction. He could have been in Nevada by now if he had kept on the trail. Slocum glanced at the powerful white stallion cropping grass. And he would never have been given such a fine horse—or lost the roan he had ridden from Colorado.

Lakshmi and elephants and nearly being killed had filled less than a week to overflowing.

"Why do you worry so about it?" asked Lakshmi.

"Don't rightly know," Slocum said, but the canyon might provide a shortcut into the Grand Tetons where they headed.

"How much farther do we have to go?"

Slocum mopped the sweat on his forehead as he studied the valley stretching ahead of them. As he put his hat back on his head a bullet jerked it from his hand and sent it flying through the air. Slocum dived for cover, shouting at Lakshmi.

The woman stood and stared at him as if he had gone crazy.

"Someone's shooting at us. Get down!"

Another shot kicked up dirt at Lakshmi's feet. This got her moving. She ran toward him, but a barrage of shots cut her off. Slocum drew his six-shooter and knew there was no point in using it. The sniper taking potshots at them used a rifle and was some distance away. The report from the rifle was muffled, and Slocum wasn't sure he even knew where the bullets were coming from.

"Stay down. I'm going after him." Slocum shoved his Colt Navy back into its holster, cast a quick, covetous glance toward his horse and the Winchester rifle resting in the saddle scabbard, then knew he could never get that far. He had to take the fight to the ambusher right away.

Keeping low, Slocum dodged back and forth amid new fire from the hidden rifleman. He reached a rockfall and caught his breath. Slocum looked back to be sure Lakshmi was staying out of the line of fire but didn't see her. He took that as good news. She was hiding and not likely to get ventilated.

Or was she?

Slocum pressed his back against the large rock and looked straight up along the curve of the boulder. He heard nothing; he saw nothing. He was sure this was the direction the shots had come from, but that didn't mean the sniper had to stay put. Slocum looked back toward where his and Lakshmi's horses nervously milled, rattling their hobbles but not panicking yet. Both had been around gunfire enough not to rear unless the slugs came mighty close.

Slocum wanted to call to Lakshmi but decided not to. He glanced upward into the rocks again and made his decision. Rather than making his way through the jagged rocks to reach the spot where the sniper had shot at them, he edged along the base of the rockfall, then cut back toward the spot where he had left Lakshmi.

On the way Slocum spotted a fresh footprint in soft dirt and knew he had been right. The sniper had taken several quick shots at them to lure Slocum away from Lakshmi, then had headed for the woman like a bee flying back to its honey hive.

Slocum slipped his six-shooter from its holster and got ready to kill. He hurried along, not worrying as much about falling into another trap as saving Lakshmi. Slocum wasn't surprised when he saw Ali holding a rifle on the woman.

Slocum gestured that Lakshmi wasn't to give any sign that he was behind the Indian servant, but she was a lousy actress. Her eyes widened, she turned toward him and said something in Hindi and gave Slocum away. Ali whirled about, his rifle blazing as he came. Bullets ricocheted off rocks and drove Slocum to cover.

"Run!" he shouted to Lakshmi. But the woman stood

frozen to the spot, whether in fear or simple indecision he could not say. All Slocum could do to help her was fire a couple rounds in Ali's direction.

"I will kill her!" shrieked Ali. "Go away. Leave us alone. You do not know what you are meddling in."

"Why don't you tell me?" Slocum began circling, angling to get a better shot at Ali. The man was clever enough to change position so any shot Slocum might take that missed its target would endanger Lakshmi.

"You cannot know. It is forbidden. I have taken an oath. Go! Leave us!"

"You'd kill the maharajah's sister?" Slocum played for time. He wanted Ali's attention split in as many ways as possible, but it didn't work. The servant ignored the wild shots Slocum sent his way and concentrated on capturing Lakshmi. He knew this was his trump card and nothing was going to sway him from taking her prisoner.

Slocum threw caution to the winds and launched a full-scale frontal assault. He pounded hard and fast to the spot where Lakshmi had stood, but the woman was nowhere to be seen. Neither was Ali. Slocum knew better than to stand in the middle of a clearing, gawking at their sudden disappearance. He flopped to the ground and wriggled like a snake until he found their footprints crushed into the tall grass. He followed fast and found them twenty yards away, at the edge of a stand of trees.

Like a prairie dog, he popped up and looked around, then went back to ground. Lakshmi made no effort to struggle or hold Ali back. Slocum cursed such bad luck on his part that she was such a willing victim. If she had kicked him or fought the least bit he could have gotten a good shot at Ali.

Slocum heard Lakshmi's voice and followed it. A loud slap silenced her, but he had the right direction now. He angled from the footprints toward the new position and knew instantly that Ali had laid a trap for him. He backpedaled and listened hard. Lakshmi made no further outbursts. That meant Ali had allowed her to call out that single time to lure Slocum.

He circled wider and came at the spot from a different direction. A man hunched over, pistol clutched in his hand. But it wasn't Ali.

"Don't move and you might live to see the sunset," Slocum said to Valande. Lakshmi's servant jumped as if ants had invaded his baggy trousers. "Drop the six-shooter," Slocum ordered sharply. He sighted in on the Indian servant and waited to squeeze off the round that would take the man's life.

Valande understood his problem and dropped the six-gun.

"You do not understand," Valande said. "I try to catch Ali. He has kidnapped my mistress."

Slocum hesitated. Valande had made a career out of spying on everyone in the maharajah's camp, especially Lakshmi.

"What are you doing out here?"

"Ali took her from the jail. I followed. I must save her from him."

Slocum lowered his six-shooter just a mite, then realized he had been tricked.

"I will shoot you, Slocum," came Ali's cold boast. "I will enjoy it. You have meddled where you were not welcome."

From the corner of his eye Slocum saw Ali had his knife to Lakshmi's slender throat. A single quick movement would behead her in a bloody fountain. Slocum turned back to Valande and saw the servant scooping up his dropped six-shooter, but it wasn't to fire at Ali. Valande pointed his pistol at Slocum.

"It is as you said, Ali," Valande said. "He is a fool. He tried to rescue her."

"Be quiet," Ali said. Lakshmi struggled a little, but Ali

drove his knife into her soft throat, bringing a tiny bead of blood to mar the flawless mahogany flesh. To Slocum, Ali said, "The map. Give me the map she stole from the rajah."

"No, John. Don't. I don't know what they want with Will Harrison but—" Lakshmi's words died in a gurgle as Ali circled her throat with his powerful arm and squeezed. Lakshmi went limp.

As Slocum started for Ali, Valande fired his pistol. The man's aim was poor and the slug ripped in front of Slocum, tearing up a patch of grass. But it was enough to stop Slocum in his tracks. That bullet could as easily have blasted out Lakshmi's heart.

"You have done well," Ali said to Valande.

Slocum watched and cried out to Valande, but he was too late. Ali drew a small pistol from the broad silk waist-band of his trousers, aimed and fired in a smooth, deliberate motion. Valande's arms rose as if on strings, then he sank straight down. Ali's bullet had caught him in the middle of the forehead and killed him instantly.

"The map," Ali said. He pointed the small pistol at Slocum. Seeing this had little effect, he pointed the gun at Lakshmi's head. The woman was still unconscious at his feet and was not going to dodge. Slocum didn't see how Ali could miss at point-blank range. Frustration rose to the point of cold hatred for the Indian servant. Slocum certainly could not cover the ground between him and the armed man before the bullet robbed Lakshmi of her life.

"What's so important about Will Harrison?" Slocum reached into his pocket and pulled out the many-times-folded map. He held it far from his body, hoping Ali's attention would focus on it rather than the more obvious target Slocum presented.

Ali sneered at such a transparent ploy and shifted the gun straight to a point in the center of Slocum's chest. Slocum twitched in anticipation of the bullet driving a hot leaden path through him.

16

Slocum figured he was a goner. He couldn't outrun a bullet, and at this distance Ali wasn't going to miss.

The sudden trumpeting of an elephant startled both men. Ali jerked about at the sound. Slocum felt the heavy footfalls of the monstrous beast through the ground under his boot soles. The instant Ali whirled and his pistol turned away from its target, he found himself contending with more than the sound of a charging elephant.

Slocum dived. He took two quick steps, launched himself and stretched out his arms to circle Ali's waist. He caught the gun hand in the cordon of his arms as he clamped down hard. Ali fought but was off-balance and staggered back. Slocum winced as a hot streak passed along his leg. Ali had fired in spite of his hand being tangled up in Slocum's embrace.

They crashed to the ground, rolling over and over. Ali's pistol discharged again, but it missed Slocum this time. He concentrated on getting his hands around the Indian's muscular throat. Try as Slocum might, he found the man too sinuous and strong. Slocum flopped away, gasping for air after Ali kicked him in the belly.

"G-get him!" Slocum pointed in the direction Ali had lit

out but the maharajah, from his vantage high on the back of the elephant in his decorated carriage box, either did not hear or chose to ignore the warning.

Slocum sat up, bent double for a moment and sucked the wind back into his lungs. He got to his feet and hurried to Lakshmi. The woman's eyelids flickered, but she didn't awaken. Slocum left her on the ground, grabbed his fallen six-shooter, then picked up the one Valande had dropped when Ali had killed him.

He looked up and swallowed hard. The maharajah had almost run him over with the charging elephant, but the gargantuan beast had stopped a few yards away. Gasim sweated heavily as he struggled with the rampaging, nervous creature. For a moment Slocum thought the elephant would toss the mahout from his perch behind the huge head, but Gasim clung tenaciously and his experience using his feet behind the ears controlled the beast's worst impulses.

"Is she hurt? I will kill him with my bare hands if that pig has harmed her!" The maharajah scrambled from the small *howdah* carrier on the elephant's back. He did not wait for Gasim to get the elephant to its knees but slid over the bulging gray side, gripped the straps and used them to lower himself.

"She's all right," Slocum said. "Did you see where Ali went?"

The maharajah knelt at Lakshmi's side and cradled her head. He looked up at Slocum.

"You saved her. Thank you for this inestimable service."

"Ali wants to kill us all," Slocum said. "Where'd the son of a bitch go? Did you see him before you came down from the elephant?"

The maharajah shrugged. "I think he went up the slope, where the elephant cannot go."

"I didn't expect to see the elephant this far up in the mountains," Slocum admitted.

"You forget your history. Hannibal crossed the Alps with an army led by war elephants."

Slocum stared blankly at the prince. He had no idea who Hannibal was, but he had heard of Hannibal, Missouri. He refrained from asking if this wasn't another of Mark Twain's wild tales.

Slocum eyed Gasim as the mahout dismounted and began tending to the elephant. The gashes on its broad gray side where the cougar had clawed it were covered with a thick yellowish paste that seemed to take any soreness or pain from the animal.

"What about him?" Slocum pointed at Gasim. "Can you trust him?"

"I have no choice," the maharajah said. "Who else can control the elephant? My other one is due to arrive soon, but until then, I am forced to use the battle-weary veteran."

"What?" Lakshmi stirred. Her brother immediately caressed her cheek. Lakshmi's eyelids fluttered.

"John?" She recoiled slightly seeing it was the maharajah who held her rather than Slocum. "I am sorry. I did not know."

"You are well, my sister. That is all that matters."

"Hate to burst your balloon," Slocum said, "but that's not all that matters. Ali is on the loose. I've got a score to settle with him."

"Is he the one?" asked Lakshmi. Seeing the maharajah's perplexed look, she added, "The one who killed his friend, Hugh Malley."

"That was an accident," the prince said. "It is of no concern."

"I—" Lakshmi started to speak but fell silent when she caught Gasim's eye. Slocum touched the six-shooter at his side and wondered how loyal the mahout was. The maharajah obviously found it difficult to believe any of his servants could turn on him. Slocum didn't bother pointing out how both Ali and Valande had tried to kill his sister.

"I'll go after him," Slocum said.

"It is not a good idea to split one's forces," the maharajah said. "We will rest before continuing on—together."

Slocum felt as if he were being pulled into the mountains after Ali. The Grand Tetons were lovely, but he wanted to add a stream of blood down their slopes. Ali couldn't escape punishment for kidnapping Lakshmi and trying to kill her. In his gut Slocum thought Ali was responsible for Hugh's death, too. The servant was the kingpin in the revolt against the prince's authority.

"Who is Will Harrison and why are you hunting for him?" Slocum addressed the question to the maharajah but looked squarely at Gasim. The mahout's impassive face might have been carved from a block of mahogany, but Slocum thought he saw a slight twitch around the eyes. Gasim knew more about this hunt than he was letting on—and certainly had a greater interest in finding Harrison than was likely for an injured elephant driver.

"This is of no concern to you," the maharajah said. "It is a matter of honor and duty."

Slocum fell silent. It sounded as if the maharajah wanted to kill Harrison. That made sense in a way, but it struck Slocum as a long way to go to carry on a blood feud. India was half the world away. Maybe on the other side of the Alps the maharajah's Hannibal had crossed.

"We rest, then we go after Will Harrison," the maharajah said firmly.

For the first time since Ali had put his pistol to Lakshmi's head, Slocum hunted for the scrap of paper Lakshmi had found in her brother's files. He hunted for it but it was gone. He didn't remember dropping it but things had been mighty hot for a spell and a tattered piece of paper had not been his primary concern.

"I will talk to Gasim about the elephant," the maharajah said. He glanced from Slocum to his sister. A look of disapproval was evident. "I shall return quickly."

"He saved my life," Lakshmi said, a little too stridently for Slocum's taste. Pleading with the maharajah wasn't the way to gain anything.

"I won't let any harm come to her," Slocum said. "On my word."

"Yes, on your word," the prince said glumly. He took Gasim by the shoulder and aimed the mahout toward the elephant, now noisily enjoying a meal of knee-high grass. When they were out of earshot, Slocum spoke to Lakshmi.

"Ali has the map. I must have dropped it when he was threatening you."

"It does not matter. I remember it well." She smiled weakly. "From my brother's viewpoint, it is all I do well."

"I wouldn't say that," Slocum said, grinning. "I hope you and him haven't been going through the *Kama Sutra* page by page together." He laughed when she blushed furiously and averted her eyes. It broke the tension and Lakshmi finally had to laugh, if a bit uncomfortably.

"You are a strange man, John Slocum. I like that."

"I'll tell you what I don't like. I don't like Ali being on the loose," Slocum said in a low voice. He saw the maharajah and Gasim completing their discussion about the elephant. Whatever was said did not set well with the prince. His expression matched the summer storms that regularly boiled over the jagged mountain peaks and came crashing down into the unsuspecting valleys.

"We can sneak away, for a while. There are so many things I must show you," Lakshmi said. "So many ways that I might repay you for saving my life."

Her brother stalked back and stood, hands balled on his hips as he glared at them.

"We must wait. The elephant is unable to continue for a few hours. By then it will be too dark to find Will Harrison."

"What of Ali?" asked Slocum.

"Pah. He is a nothing. An outcast. A *mieccha*!"

"What's that?" asked Slocum. "Sounds as bad as calling a gent a lily-livered, no account snake in the grass."

"Worse," Lakshmi said. "It is the castless of our society. The untouchable. No one has anything to do with them. They are beneath contempt and notice."

"We will find Will Harrison in the morning," the maharajah said decisively, as if this made it so. He struck a fine pose, but to Slocum that was all it was. Bluster and show for Lakshmi's sake and nothing more.

"You have a map for finding him?" Slocum saw a slight smile twitch the man's lips as he looked at his sister. He knew she had stolen the map from his files.

"I have the real one," he said softly. Reaching into his jacket, he pulled out a sheet of paper identical to the other, but from the quick look Slocum got, he saw significant differences. Slocum let out a little sigh of relief. The map Ali had was a fake, a decoy the prince had planted in his belongings against such a theft.

"I am not so stupid after all, eh, Mr. Slocum?"

"Never said you were," Slocum replied but that had been exactly what had crossed his mind. He looked over his shoulder in Gasim's direction and said in a whisper, "What of him? Can he be trusted?"

"Gasim? No more than the others," the maharajah said. "And no less. He is a loyal retainer. He is from Afghanistan, a *wilavatis*. What the British call a mercenary."

"So he's likely to sell out to the highest bidder? What can Ali offer him that you can't?"

"You go on so about Ali. Forget him. He is untouchable. His name will never again pass your lips."

Slocum wasn't going to argue the point. Knowing that Gasim had fought for money made it all the more likely he could be bought. As rich as the maharajah looked, he didn't seem the kind to spread the wealth around among his hired hands.

"I'll pitch my bedroll over yonder," Slocum said, pointing to a clump of trees some distance away.

"What am I to do for my tent?" asked the maharajah. Seeing Slocum's expression, he suddenly grinned and said, "Ah, the American reluctance to serve one's better. That is all right. Lakshmi can pitch it."

"What about Gasim? If you offer him enough, he'll likely do it." The sarcasm was lost on the prince.

"He must tend the elephant. The beast's wounds are substantial and must be tended and permitted to heal properly. I do wish the other elephant had arrived before we left Hoback Junction."

"How many of those elephants do you have?" Slocum asked.

"Many. I am a mighty king of the Rajput."

"He is only a rajah," Lakshmi said, "but already he thinks of the day when our father is gone and he is a real maharajah."

"Be quiet, woman," the prince said.

"Where's your gear?" Slocum asked, cutting off a tirade. "I'll pitch your tent for you."

With ill grace the maharajah showed Slocum how the gear had been stowed in the elephant carriage. The tent was light and easily handled until a breeze kicked up, blowing down forcefully from the upper slopes. Slocum's sharp sense of smell caught a hint of rain on the wind, but he could not decide if they were in for a sudden shower or if he was only catching the edge of a storm on the far side of the mountains.

"The silk is quite waterproof," Lakshmi said, helping him with the ropes holding the tent upright. "It is a fine material."

"Makes better shirts than tents," Slocum said. "I won a silk shirt off a gambler in San Francisco once. I had to get a tailor to let out the shoulders but it wore real good."

"Do you still have it?"

Slocum shook his head. He had gotten a lot of blood on it—none of it his—and had found it impossible to remove. He had buried it with the owlhoot who had tried to kill him with a hunting knife.

"I will see that you get another. One with the royal insignia of Rajasthan on it."

She laid a hand on his arm and looked up at him from beneath her long dark lashes. Slocum started to tell her to wait until her brother had bedded down for the night and then he would bed her, but tiny sights and sounds came to him that brought him around.

"What is it, John?"

"I don't know." He slid his six-shooter from its holster and took a couple steps in the direction of the temporary elephant corral. "Stop!" he shouted. Slocum brought the six-gun up and fired in a smooth motion, but the range was too great for him to hope to hit Ali.

"John, no!" Lakshmi tried to hold him back. He jerked free.

"They've got your brother. Ali and Gasim, the son of a bitch. In cahoots!"

He had been right about the mahout, and it galled him he had not been able to convince the maharajah to watch his back better. At a dead run, Slocum got to the spot where Gasim had penned the elephant by simply digging a shallow trench around it. Slocum remembered that elephants could not jump, but this looked too easy. Why didn't the elephant simply step across it?

All such thoughts vanished when he saw Ali dragging the maharajah off. The prince was not putting up much of a fight.

"Let him go!"

Ali took a quick shot with his small-bore pistol. Slocum didn't even flinch at the soft *pop!* when it discharged. He tried to get a good shot at Ali, but the man used the maharajah as a shield, forcing Slocum to get closer or risk killing the man he tried to rescue.

"There, there they are!" shouted Gasim.

Slocum spun, leveled his pistol and fired at the mahout. Gasim threw up his uninjured hand in surprise, then dodged into the woods and fled. Slocum hesitated. He could go after the mahout, but Ali had the prince.

By the time he returned to the trail, Ali and his kidnap victim had disappeared.

Slocum backed toward camp, then reluctantly went to fetch his horse only to find a desolate Lakshmi standing and staring at him.

"The horses," she said in a choked voice. "They are gone. Stolen!"

"Ali's smarter and sneakier than I gave him credit for," Slocum said in disgust. "And he's got your brother."

"With the real map," Lakshmi said.

Slocum had no answer for that. He had made one bad decision after another today, and now a man's life hung in the balance. He turned slowly and stared at the elephant in its crude pen.

"What the hell?" Slocum said. "What's one more blunder?" He grabbed Lakshmi's hand and pulled her along. "Show me how to steer that damned thing," he said.

"What thing is that?" She dug her heels in and stared at him in disbelief as it dawned on her what he intended doing.

"The elephant," he said, confirming her worst fears. "How do we saddle up and ride that elephant?"

17

"He would die before he gave any information to Ali," Lakshmi said. She saw Slocum's expression and got mad. "My brother is destined to be a king one day, possibly someday soon. He is of noble caste and places honor above all else."

"Maybe so," Slocum allowed, "but I suspect Ali can get mighty persuasive. There are things Indians do with knives that no man—" Slocum broke off his angry tirade when he saw her face. "I meant Plains Indians. Sioux. Crow. Arapaho and Cheyenne."

"We have evil men who also know how to torture, but Ali is not of their caste. He is evil but does not possess such knowledge."

"It doesn't take much to figure out how to make a man scream if you don't care if he lives after you're finished," Slocum said. He stopped at the edge of the shallow trench Gasim had dug and stared at the elephant. The gray mountain of flesh bellowed loudly, raising its trunk high and looking the world like it meant to stomp on him. Slocum uneasily looked down at the shallow trench and wondered if such a small pit would contain its fury. He would have preferred to be standing on the north rim of the Grand Canyon looking at the elephant on the south rim.

"If only the horses had not been taken," Lakshmi said. "We could go after them right away."

"I suspect Gasim had a hand in that," Slocum said.

"But he never left the elephant's side," Lakshmi said. "Every time I looked, he was here."

"You weren't always looking at Gasim," Slocum said.

"I did look at you. A little." Again the shyly averted eyes contrasted so with her bold sexuality. "But I am sure Gasim did not leave the elephant." Now Lakshmi's voice rang with conviction.

Slocum wasn't inclined to argue. How Gasim had crept about and made off with the horses so Ali could nab the maharajah was something of a mystery that could wait to be solved later. Right now he was faced with four tons of angry elephant.

"Might be I could follow Ali on foot," Slocum said uneasily.

"Are you not the mighty bronco buster? That is the term, is it not?"

Slocum was stung by Lakshmi's sarcasm. He settled his Colt Navy, made sure the leather keeper was securely snugged down over the hammer to keep it from bouncing out of the holster, then stepped across the shallow ditch and was on the same side as the elephant. They were on an island of dirt in the middle of the vast Grand Tetons, and Slocum had never felt more alone. He stared up at the massive beast and was encouraged when it did not charge him. It had two short, yellowed ivory tusks capped with gold balls to prevent the elephant from inflicting serious injury on its handler.

Slocum shivered as he stepped closer. A toss of that great head and the lightest brush of a tusk would send him flying through the air, body broken and on his way to being entirely dead. He wished he could sell those tusks to some piano company for keys, *then* approach the towering gray brute.

He took another careful step forward, remembering this was the beast that had stomped on Hugh Malley and crushed the life from his body as easily as a man might snuff out a match.

"The elephant is a gentle soul," Lakshmi said from behind him. "Take the long pole, the one with the hook, and approach him. Tap him on the side of the head to turn him, then apply the shaft forcefully behind his knees to get him to kneel so you can mount."

"Sounds easy enough," Slocum said. He was sweating but he was not as frightened as he had thought he might be this close to the elephant. What Lakshmi said seemed true. The elephant showed little fear of him. This was no supernatural wendigo. It was flesh and blood, and Gasim had controlled it as easily as Slocum rode a horse. If the mercenary could do it, so could Slocum. He had worked with all kinds of animals in his day, although never one this large.

Doing as Lakshmi suggested, he found it easy enough to get the elephant to turn the way he wanted, but when he swung the pole and whacked it loudly behind the front knees, it bellowed and tried to rear. Its trunk lashed out like a thick whip and the deadly tusks forced Slocum to retreat.

"The hook! Use the hook!" Lakshmi cried. "Do not let it behave this way toward you!"

Slocum reacted instinctively and caught the elephant's large flapping ear with the hook. Using both hands on the pole, he pulled hard. Both his feet left the ground as the elephant tossed its head, but Slocum hung on and hit the ground again. He kept pulling on the hook until the elephant settled down.

"That's working," he said in surprise. He tried to swing the pole to tap the elephant's knees again but didn't have to. The elephant was already dropping down clumsily.

"Now we can go," Lakshmi said brightly. She jumped

the ditch and came over, scrambling up the side of the elephant into the ornate carriage. The *howdah* leaned precariously as she entered and finally settled down.

"Don't get too comfortable," Slocum said. "You have to leave me some room."

"But, John, you are the mahout. You ride on the neck."

Slocum stared at the still-obedient elephant and knew he had to move fast or he'd lose his nerve. He took a running jump and shinnied agilely so he could straddle the elephant's neck, feet dangling on either side. His boots pressed into the backsides of the elephant's floppy ears, and he wondered about using his spurs.

Then it was all he could do to hang on. A rope around the elephant's neck provided a halter for him to grip, and this kept him from being tossed off as the beast regained its feet.

"How do we get it out of its pen?"

"I put down rocks and brushed dirt over them. There is a bridge," Lakshmi called from the carriage. "The elephant will walk across it with no problem. Now quit talking. Find my brother!" The imperial command in her voice would have offended Slocum had he not been working so hard to steer the elephant where he wanted it to go. The beast saw the dirt bridge and crossed it quickly, letting out a triumphant bellow before breaking into a trot.

"How do I slow it down?" Slocum asked. He had no bit and bridle to control the elephant. Worse than not having any way of keeping the elephant's speed down, the sun was now setting behind the towering mountains and turning the landscape into an eerie twilight when viewed from this elevation.

"I do not know. You are the mahout. Do whatever a mahout does," Lakshmi said unhelpfully. "I will keep the lookout for my brother. That is the expression, isn't it?"

Slocum didn't answer. He used the hooked pole to tap

on one side of the elephant's head and then the other as he felt his way to a better control. He figured he knew how to get more speed from the elephant, but that wasn't what he wanted in the gathering gloom of dusk.

"To the right," called Lakshmi. "They are riding down an arroyo. A rocky ravine. I see them. My brother looks to be hurt!"

Slocum was getting the hang of controlling the elephant and steered it down into the draw. The elephant liked the sandy, small-pebbled ravine floor better than the more heavily rock-strewn path above. Legs reaching out, the elephant more than matched the speed of Ali's horse. When the maharajah began stirring, Slocum thought they had a chance of overtaking the kidnapper.

What would happen then he didn't know. Ali could kill the maharajah with a single slash of a knife or bullet to the brain. Slocum had his Colt, which was unsuitable for long-distance shooting, but he might spook Ali's horses and throw them off stride. He was willing to do anything because he had no idea how much longer his luck would hold and he would remain in control of the elephant.

"Does the elephant respond to voice commands?" Slocum called back to Lakshmi.

"I do not know. The mahout always speaks in low tones so the passengers are not disturbed."

Slocum grumbled under his breath. Gasim probably had taught the elephant a long list of words to control it, but Slocum knew none of them and doubted his cuss words would affect the huge beast one way or the other. He looked up to see Ali's horse beginning to turn skittish at the rapid approach of the elephant.

Slocum drew his six-gun and fired a single round for effect. He wanted to know if the elephant would react as much as he wanted Ali to get down and make a stand. The maharajah was tossed belly down over Slocum's white stallion and stirred weakly. From what Slocum could tell, the prince's hands were bound and he was lashed into place. The maharajah would be no help in getting himself free.

The weight of the rescue fell entirely on Slocum's shoulders.

Slocum did what he could to direct the elephant to Ali, but there was no way he could stop the rampaging beast. The elephant shot past Ali, but Slocum did succeed in getting between the kidnapper and his victim.

"Can you get down and go to your brother?" Slocum called but knew that wasn't possible. The elephant continued down the ravine at top speed. Lakshmi would be dead in a thrice if she tried to dismount now.

"John, there, look!"

Slocum craned his head around and saw Gasim running for the maharajah. His face glowed with rivers of sweat in the early night starlight, showing the intense effort he had made getting here from the spot where the prince had been kidnapped. Slocum couldn't imagine how hard and fast Gasim had run to match both horse and elephant.

"What's he yelling?"

"I cannot make it out," Lakshmi said.

Slocum did what he could to get the elephant turned around. It took close to a quarter mile to swing the ponderous beast about by using his feet on the ears and whacking with the hooked pole, but once he aimed back up the ravine, the elephant began its wild charge again. It had only two speeds. Dead stop and all-out.

As the elephant trampled its way back along the draw, Slocum leaned over and fired several times at Gasim, who was trying to do something to the maharajah. The mahout looked up in surprise and shouted something in Hindi. Then the elephant was past.

"John, he is trying to help. He is not with Ali!"

"What?" Slocum struggled to control the elephant's

charge again. The beast trumpeted noisily, sending echoes up and down the mountains.

"Gasim is helping my brother! He said to tell the elephant *chota*."

"What's that mean?"

"Little. I think it tells the elephant to slow, to not go so fast!"

Slocum began shouting the command as he leaned back, as if he were in the saddle of a quarter horse working to rope a calf. To his surprise, the elephant slowed it headlong pace and then came to a halt.

"Not going to try steering any more," Slocum said. He slid to one side, grabbed a floppy ear and then let himself down to the ground. The elephant glared at him for the ear pull but remained standing and stationary.

Slocum ran back to where Gasim worked to get the maharajah free of the ropes binding him to the stallion. The mahout was having little luck because Ali fired sporadically, forcing Gasim to return fire. The nearness of flying lead spooked the stallion, causing Gasim to divide his attention three different ways. When Slocum arrived, the odds changed.

Reaching down, Slocum pulled out the thick-bladed knife he carried in his right boot top. A quick slash severed the ropes holding the maharajah and sent the prince crashing to the ground. He groaned and his dark eyes fixed on Slocum, but the glare was more damning for the fall than thankful for releasing him from bondage.

"Get him to the elephant and clear out. Take Lakshmi with you."

"You can do nothing against Ali. He is a maniac," Gasim said, panting harshly.

Slocum worked to reload his Colt Navy. He led his rearing stallion away to where it would be out of the line of fire while Gasim helped the prince. The maharajah's feet were still tied, forcing him to hop clumsily. Gasim muttered constantly. Maybe it was encouragement or maybe it was something more vitriolic. Whatever the mahout said, it kept the prince moving and out of Ali's sights.

"Get to the elephant," Slocum said. "I'll hold him down." With a steady fire into the clump of bushes where he thought Ali was hiding, Slocum made sure the renegade servant could not get a decent shot at his prince.

Slocum saw Gasim order the elephant to drop to its knees and boost the maharajah into the carriage with Lakshmi. The mahout jumped to the elephant's neck and positioned himself, making *hut-hut-hut* noises to urge the elephant to greater speed.

The elephant awkwardly rose, then started back up the draw at a speed that amazed Slocum. What the elephant did, it did well.

He turned his attention back to the bushes but saw no movement. He might have gotten in a lucky shot and killed Ali, but his gut didn't tell him that. As Slocum began a slow sneak toward the spot where he thought Ali had taken refuge, he heard a single shot ring out.

The *pop!* matched that of the small pistol Ali had—but it didn't come from ahead. Slocum swung about and saw Gasim throw up his hands and begin to wobble. Ali's shot had hit the mahout.

And the elephant was charging along at full speed again with Lakshmi and her brother helpless in the carriage.

Slocum rammed his six-gun back into the holster and sprinted for his horse. He had to stop the rampaging elephant somehow. He hoped something occurred to him before he got up to it because he was as dry of ideas as the Mojave was of water in the middle of summer.

With a loud Rebel yell, he put his spurs to his stallion's flanks and raced off, hoping he could rescue Lakshmi and her brother.

Somehow.

18

Slocum kept the horse plunging up the arroyo at a break-neck speed even the elephant could not match. Slocum pulled even and looked up. Gasim hung precariously, flopping about as the elephant loped along out of control.

"Are you all right?" He tried to see if Lakshmi and the maharajah were still in the carriage but couldn't spot them. He hadn't passed them in the ravine so they must still be crouching inside the *howdah*, trying to stay out of sight and Ali's line of fire.

Slocum pushed his stallion closer to the elephant with its rapidly driving long legs. The horse tried to balk, but Slocum kept after it until he came to a rope halter dangling from around the elephant's neck. He took a deep breath then cast caution to the winds. Kicking free of his stirrups, he launched himself across the divide between horse and elephant. His grasping fingers caught the hemp rope. For a brief instant he felt it slipping through his grip, then he clamped down hard enough to swing about. He crashed into the side of the elephant, disturbing its rhythm. The elephant bellowed in surprise and anger and began to slow as it tried to pull him free using its powerful trunk.

Slocum clambered up the side of the great beast, hurting it as he dug spurs into the tough gray hide. Slocum hated to injure the elephant further, but it was either that or be flung off. Slocum didn't want to die, and he didn't want to sacrifice the maharajah and Lakshmi, either. Grimly climbing, he came to the spot where Gasim was tangled up in rope. The man was dead. His sightless eyes gave no hint what he saw on the other side. Slocum vowed not to join him to find out anytime soon.

Pushing Gasim back, he sat in front of the mahout and began shouting the single word he knew.

"*Chota, chota!*" The elephant had endured enough punishment for the day and obeyed. Slowly, ever so slowly, it obeyed until Slocum sat astride the massive head on a completely stationary creature.

"John? John!"

Slocum glanced over his shoulder and saw Lakshmi hanging over the edge of the carriage.

"Get your brother out. Can he move?"

"We need to dismount when the elephant is kneeling. It is only fitting for a rajah and—" Lakshmi quieted when she saw the fire in his eyes. Slocum cared nothing for the perquisites due royalty. He wanted off and away from this mountain of a creature before it took it into its head to trumpet its pain and rage and race off again.

"I'll see what I can do," Lakshmi said.

"Hurry it up." Slocum swiveled about and tried to untangle Gasim from the rope around the elephant's neck. Failing, he used his knife to sever the rope. The dead mahout crashed to the ground. This sight as much as Slocum's goading got Lakshmi to help the maharajah out of the carriage.

"No!" she shrieked as the prince slipped from her grip. He slid over the bulging gray side and flopped hard onto the ground. Lakshmi quickly followed, landing heavily and sitting beside her brother, rubbing her ankle. She glared up at Slocum.

He slid his leg over the top of the elephant's head and dropped the fifteen feet to the ground. The impact shook him, but he was ready for it and hit with bent knees. He stumbled a few steps and then came up, looking around for any sign of Ali.

"You can't let the elephant go," the maharajah said. "Not until I get my other one in from Cheyenne."

It was too late. The elephant took it into its head to go exploring, and Slocum let it go without trying to stop it. He was fed up with dealing with the monster.

"You did well for someone with no training," the maharajah said. "You should train to, uh, wrangle elephants. I will hire you and take you back to India!"

"Like hell," Slocum said. He dusted himself off, then saw that Lakshmi was all right. Her ankle was a little swollen, but she was able to walk on it if she did not try to go too fast. Slocum fixed her a rude crutch out of a fallen piñon branch before turning to the maharajah.

"You owe me an explanation," Slocum said. "What's Will Harrison to you and why is Ali so eager to kill you to keep you from getting to him?"

"I do not know Ali's motives," the maharajah said, "but I have sworn an oath that binds me by honor."

"What's your beef with Harrison?"

The maharajah pulled himself upright against a tree, took a deep breath and then launched into his story.

"His father, the Lord of Swansea, was a noted soldier in India. Unlike many of the British officers, he worked with my people and did not impose his will unreasonably. While it is going too far to say he was beloved, he was certainly respected."

"By you?" asked Slocum.

"I loved the man like a father," the maharajah said. "He saved my life and he worked for seventeen years to keep my father in power as maharajah. If possible, Lord Swansea is family to all of us."

Slocum glanced at Lakshmi and saw her nodding in agreement. A small smile curled her lips that said more than words might. She shared her brother's assessment of the British soldier.

"What has Lord Swansea asked of you?" Lakshmi watched with wide eyes. Slocum was a little surprised that the woman really did not know why her brother had made the trip to America.

"He is dying of wounds. His oldest son, Robert, was killed in the same ambush." The maharajah looked as if he would spit when he added, "They killed all the thugs who ambushed them. Their fate was too swift."

"So you're here to tell Will Harrison his father's dying?" Slocum scratched his head at this. A telegram would have served the same purpose, or a courier since Harrison seemed to be sequestered in the middle of the Grand Tetons doing whatever he did.

"Will is a remittance man and receives his stipend every month. If that were all, it would be easy to send along a letter to him. No, this is far more serious."

Slocum held his tongue so the maharajah could get to the answer in his own fashion. From the dreamy look on the prince's face, it might take a spell.

"I have sworn *rakhri* in this matter. This means I am obligated to perform a service in return for the years of loyalty."

"But, my brother," protested Lakshmi, "*rakhri* is an obligation of the entire family. You never told me!"

"I am sorry for that," the maharajah said. "I thought to make this a swift journey and an enjoyable one. I selfishly wanted to hunt the buffalo and bear and the mountain lion to return to India so I could brag about it. But more than this, I wanted to return to tell Lord Swansea that his second son had been informed that he was soon to inherit the family estates."

Slocum suddenly understood. The maharajah had said

the lord's oldest son had been killed. By the British laws of primogeniture only the oldest son inherited the family title and estates. With Robert Harrison dead, that meant Will was now fabulously wealthy and no longer had to be sent his monthly pittance to keep him from becoming an annoyance. He had gone from remittance man to wealthy lord in one ambush somewhere in India.

"I can see why this should be news delivered in person," Slocum said. "Harrison wouldn't likely believe it otherwise."

"We have also met, so we will be able to recognize each other. I intended to make a present to him of the white elephant. Such a gesture would affirm my message. For a short while, Will Harrison was a soldier in the British Army, although he quickly proved himself less than adequate for the position. Lord Swansea placed young Will under my tutelage, but while we became friends, he never learned the basics of soldiering."

Slocum wondered if the maharajah was half as good a soldier as he made himself out to be. He might be, but the way his own servants had turned on him belied that. Still, he had kept the mercenary Gasim loyal to him even as Valande and Ali betrayed him.

The maharajah pushed back his sleeve and showed a braided ropy bracelet knotted around his left wrist.

"This is the *rakhri* band symbolizing my duty. Any of my family who see it must help." The maharajah laughed short and hard, almost a barking sound. "Of course I come to a country where there are none of my extensive family to help me, other than my own dear sister." He bowed slightly in Lakshmi's direction.

"And you said nothing of this," Lakshmi said. Her hot eyes bored into her brother's. She was not happy with him, but Slocum guessed even a sister did not show too much anger toward a man who would one day be the king of his country.

"I thought it was a simple chore, one quickly finished. That is why I took so much time crossing Wyoming."

"You're supposed to take Will Harrison back with you?"

"If he will come. His father's injuries are serious. Even if he survives, he will linger for years. He will need his heir at his side to take over the reins of power, to run the considerable estates in both India and England and to perform the social functions of a Lord of Swansea."

"What if he likes it here and doesn't want to go with you?"

The prince looked surprised. "I never considered that. Why, of course he will accept the title. It is his role in life, his duty, his karma." He looked at Slocum as if Slocum's suggestion was the stupidest thing he had ever heard in his life.

Slocum wondered. The few remittance men he had known personally were ne'er-do-wells who lacked any ambition, but one of the reasons for that was their easy life out West. They got enough money to live on, which allowed them to gamble, whore, drink and indulge themselves in any outrageous behavior that occurred to them or their disreputable friends. One or two had made fortunes on their own. Slocum thought of a remittance man in Montana who had used his trickle of funds from his father to buy and build a cattle ranch that stretched a quarter million acres. He might be richer than his father by now. But he was decidedly a different sort of man and not like most of the remittance men Slocum had known.

Why would Will Harrison return to England or even India if his life here was easy and pleasant?

"What's Harrison doing in the mountains? Mining?"

"I believe that is so," the maharajah said. "I don't see your point."

"What if he's hit it big? Gold or silver can make a man a millionaire overnight. Letting packs of dogs rip apart a fox or taking afternoon tea might not be Harrison's idea of a good time anymore."

"He *must* return," the prince said. "It is his duty."

Slocum saw that honor and duty were everything for the maharajah. He understood the powerful tug. While his own family had been alive, he would have done anything for them. Anything. During the war, he had ridden with some of the most vicious murderers on either side of the Mason-Dixon Line and felt closer to them than he did to most folks. They had been a kind of family—or something more, something different but no less powerfully binding.

"You don't have any idea why Ali and Valande were trying to stop you?" Slocum thought on that a moment, then added, "Ali wanted to reach Harrison before you. Why'd he want to do a thing like that?" He knew the answer if not Ali's motive. The Indian servant wanted to kill Will Harrison.

"They were evil men," Lakshmi said. That satisfied her and her brother, but Slocum wanted more. Ali and Valande had trusted positions as servants to a powerful Indian prince. Why sacrifice their lives unless the reward was far greater than any power they might gain working for the future king?

"Ali is still on the loose," Slocum said, "but there's no way to run him down now. He's had considerable time to make himself scarce." He thought for a moment, then asked, "I don't know what became of the map Lakshmi took. You said it was a fake."

"I suspected someone in my camp of wanting to find the map," the maharajah explained, "but I had never thought my own sister would take the map. It was, as you said, bogus. I have the real map here." He patted a pocket, got a strange expression and began fumbling about. "That's odd. It is missing. The map's gone!" He looked at Slocum and held out his hands, palms up, in a gesture of helplessness.

"Any idea what happened to it? Did Ali get it?"

"I don't think so. When would he have taken it? I must have dropped it during the scuffle."

"You don't seem too worried," Slocum said. "Can you find Harrison without the map?"

The maharajah tapped his forehead and smiled.

"I have the information etched here. It is something Will's father taught me. A mere glance at a map will give me full knowledge of it for all time."

Slocum looked at the dark sky and knew that trying to find Will Harrison now was out of the question.

"We'll be off first thing in the morning," he said. "We're going to need some transportation. I've got my horse but—"

"But nothing," Lakshmi said. "Look, the elephant has returned, so we have it also. My brother can ride the horse and you can be my mahout." She grinned broadly at his discomfort at the notion.

"You want me to steer the elephant again? No," Slocum said. "I'm not getting on that monster again. There's no way you can make me. It's too big and too ornery. I can't make it do what I want, either, since it doesn't understand English."

They hit the trail the next morning, the maharajah riding the majestic white stallion and Slocum once more atop the huge elephant.

19

Slocum would never enjoy riding an elephant. The motion was all wrong and nothing compared with a decent horse for going up narrow mountain roads. He kept glancing at the maharajah, riding high, wide and fancy free on the white stallion, and almost envied the man. Almost. The prince had a whale of a lot to do, telling Will Harrison of his brother's death and his father's approaching death. Slocum didn't know how much the news would be leavened by Harrison learning he was going to be the next Lord Swansea. Receiving a white elephant as a gift hardly made the news any more palatable.

This set Slocum to thinking in other directions. Ali's attacks had a focus to them that centered on Will Harrison. Slocum couldn't figure what the maharajah's former servant gained by killing the remittance man.

"There," called the maharajah. "This is the trail leading to Harrison's mine."

"I'm not so sure I can get the elephant up there," Slocum said. He looked down uneasily at the trunk snaking back toward him. He and the elephant were getting along better now, but he lacked the experience to keep it under control if it took off at full speed. Maneuvering up the narrow trail into what might be a box canyon amounted to suicide from where Slocum sat atop the elephant.

"I can go talk to him," the maharajah said. "The mine is only a few miles farther."

"What of me?" called Lakshmi.

"Stay with Mr. Slocum," her brother shouted. He waved, put his heels to the stallion's flanks and rocketed up the trail. "I shan't be long before returning with Will Harrison."

Slocum looked at Lakshmi and smiled.

"How long do you reckon your brother'll be?" Slocum asked.

"One page, at least. Perhaps two." Lakshmi's hot dark eyes fixed on him. He knew instantly what she meant, and it didn't matter which pages from the *Kama Sutra* they chose.

Slocum kicked and prodded and called to the elephant and, to his surprise, got the elephant to kneel so Lakshmi could dismount.

"Wish I knew how I did that," Slocum said, sliding down to the ground. Lakshmi looked at him, licked her lips and stepped closer. Her silken clothing flowed with the gentle wind blowing through the Grand Tetons, pressing the soft cloth sensuously against her body.

"It does not matter as long as you know how to do other things," she said.

"Never had a problem getting mounted," he said. She came into the circle of his arms, pressing her lithe body warmly against his. Their lips met, and Slocum was taken away from the world of the smelly, trumpeting elephant and deadly servants and lost remittance men sought by Indian maharajahs. All that mattered was held in his arms. Lakshmi's breasts crushed hard against his chest in their embrace. Through the soft silken blouse she wore, he felt her nipples beginning to harden into tight points. This pushed his own passions up even more.

"I don't have a blanket to spread for us," he said as he broke off their deep kiss.

"One is not needed."

"Another page out of your love manual?"

"Why, yes," Lakshmi said impishly. "Or are you asking for manual love?" She reached down and unfastened his gun belt and then deftly worked on the buttons fastening his jeans. She caught the fleshy stalk sprouting up from his groin and began running her fingers up and down its hardening length. Every touch was electric and sent tingles of pure joy into Slocum's body. He gasped when her magic touch slipped lower and cupped him. She squeezed and pinched and soothed and stimulated fantastically all at the same time. Slocum snapped to rigid attention like a new recruit on parade for the first time.

"So nice," cooed Lakshmi, "but it does neither of us any good here."

"How—?"

Slocum was quickly suffocated with her kisses again. Lakshmi pushed him backward until his back was up against a post oak tree. Trapped between her passion and the hard wood trunk, Slocum found himself unsure what to do. Lakshmi seemed to know exactly what she wanted, however, and did it.

Her kisses turned softer, subtler as they moved from his lips down to the throbbing rigidity of his manhood. Here she lavished great care on him, her tongue and teeth alternating with her lips to soothe and stimulate. She nipped and kissed, licked and breathed her heavenly hot breath across his aroused flesh until Slocum felt like a skyrocket ready to detonate in the Fourth of July sky.

He let her have her way, running his hands through her silken raven-dark hair. It flowed like water under his hands. He pushed it away so he could see her face as she worked so eagerly at his groin. The sight of the woman's obvious enjoyment from what she did coupled with the feelings lancing into him almost set him off.

Lakshmi sensed this and did *things* to give him a chance to catch his breath and regain control.

"You're too good," he said. Sweat beaded his face now. He wasn't sure how much longer he wanted the Indian princess doing this to him, for him. He wanted to return the pleasures she gave him—and greedily he wanted more for himself, as well.

She looked up. The stark erotic desire graven on her lovely face told Slocum she was enjoying this, too, but he wanted to move on. Maybe he was a pushy American, but he was getting enough of the subtle Indian ways of lovemaking.

"Come on, Lakshmi. Now," he insisted.

"I agree," she said. She stood and began rustling her clothing as she shifted the flowing silks and curtains of gold and pearls that decorated her. Slocum saw her legs flash like teak in the Wyoming sun and then she swarmed up on him so quickly it took his breath away again. Lakshmi's arms circled his neck and her legs wrapped about his waist. He was pushed backward hard against the tree, but more important, he felt the fleecy triangle nestled between her legs opening for his manly probe.

Lakshmi wiggled her hips until he felt her nether lips parting in a lewd kiss on the very tip of his manstalk. Satisfied with this for a moment, Lakshmi kissed him with increasing fervor. When he was ready to demand more, she gave it. Her hips lowered, pressing him completely against the tree trunk. She continued her gentle positioning as he slid easily into her well-moistened slit.

Slocum felt as if he balanced on the edge of the world. He supported her entire body but there was little strain. Braced as he was against the tree, he could take her weight with no problem. Her sleek, strong legs tensed and pulled her hips down. As she relaxed, she slipped away. The movement was small, deliberate, unlike the powerful thrusting that appealed so to Slocum. But the agitation built tensions within him that were akin to those he got being completely in control.

Lakshmi moved about in a corkscrewing motion, back and forth just a little, always spinning about as she moved with increasing zeal. The silks wrapping her body fluttered like bright banners in the afternoon sun but neither of them saw. Both worked furiously with their eyes clamped tightly shut.

Slocum fought to keep control to eke out just a little more pleasure before he exploded like a stick of dynamite. And Lakshmi performed minor miracles with her tiny motions that stirred both body and soul. She paused a moment as only her fluttering pinkly scalloped nether gates touched the end of his shaft. Then she thrust down with speed and determination that matched any Slocum could have mustered.

He felt suddenly surrounded by her warm clinging flesh. The moistness oozed around his thick fleshly plug and dribbled downward, tickling as it went. But the sensations mounted rapidly and such small details were easily overlooked. He concentrated on the waves of heat blasting downward into his loins, ricocheting and returning up the entire length of his manhood.

With hips wiggling, twisting and striving, Lakshmi let out a low groan of sheer pleasure. Seconds later Slocum joined her in carnal release. He clung tightly to her until all his muscles turned to jelly. He sank down the tree trunk, the woman ending up resting in his lap with her legs on either side and a huge flow of silks all about.

"What page was that?" Slocum asked. "I surely did like it."

"There are footnotes," Lakshmi said, grinning. "I can—"

She jerked about when a gunshot echoed from far up in the canyon. Three more rapidly followed. Slocum lifted her bodily, stood and put her onto her feet. He was buttoning himself up as he went to fetch his six-gun where Lakshmi had left it in the grass a few delightful minutes earlier.

"What is happening?" Lakshmi put her hand to her lips when three more shots sounded. One was a throatier roar, like a shotgun, but it was quickly followed by the smaller *pops!*

"Sounds like a gunfight," Slocum said. "Mostly, it sounds like Ali's doing all the firing."

"What are we going to do?"

Slocum saw the elephant contentedly grabbing tall grass with its trunk, pulling the plant from the ground and then stuffing it into its mouth. Nothing was going to budge that creature, and even if Slocum could get it headed in the right direction there was scant room for it along the narrow trail leading back into the canyon to Will Harrison's claim.

"On foot. It's the only way. Stay here," he said as he started up the trail.

"That's my brother! I want to go!"

"You don't have a gun," Slocum said, wondering what argument would work with a princess. "Besides, you have to watch the elephant. It'll likely be our only transportation back to Hoback Junction."

He saw Lakshmi was torn between duty to the elephant and seeing what happened to her brother. Slocum gave her no time to think. He kissed her hard, gently pushed her in the direction of the grazing elephant and said, "I'll be back quicker 'n a flash."

He left that fast, legs pumping hard to get up the slope so he would be out of Lakshmi's sight in minutes. The longer she watched him the more likely she was to try and tag along and make what was a bad situation a whole lot worse. Slocum kept hoping to hear the shotgun's report as he trudged up the increasingly steep trail into the mountains, but it did not come. If it had, that meant Will Harrison was putting up a fight. The single blast from the scattergun might carry some hope if there had not been any pistol shots afterward. There had been, so Harrison had not killed Ali.

Puffing like a steam engine, Slocum had to take a rest. He looked at the winding trail behind, almost expecting to see Lakshmi. She had said India had mountainous regions and she was comfortable in them, but she remained with the elephant.

At least Slocum hoped that she did.

He settled his hat on his head, checked his Colt Navy, then continued on the road winding around the mountainside until he came to a sign nailed on a pine tree proclaiming this to be "Harrison's Hole."

Slocum's heart leapt with joy when he heard the bass roar of the shotgun again. He sprinted up the trail, rounding a bend and finally seeing the shaft sunk into the side of the mountain. Tailings had been puked out like some vile gray stream halfway down the mountainside into a deep arroyo. To one side stood a line shack, now ventilated with new holes in the sides. Slocum looked around and saw a tall, husky man clutching the shotgun as he peered around the edge of the shack. He looked in the direction of the mineshaft, but Slocum saw the danger coming from a different direction.

"Will! Behind you!" he shouted. It was too far for Slocum to get a good shot, even if he could have sent the lead accurately whining past Will Harrison's ear. Ali rushed up from behind the miner and smashed him in the head with a rock.

As Harrison fell, Slocum began firing. His slugs tore more splinters from the side of the shack, but they also forced Ali to duck low to avoid having his head blown off.

"Give up, Ali. You can't get away."

"I killed Hugh Malley, I'll kill Harrison and the maharajah *and* you, Slocum!" Ali knelt as he broke open his small pistol and fumbled for rounds in his pockets.

Slocum gave him no time to reload. He rushed ahead, firing as he went. Ali realized he was a sitting duck and jammed the unloaded pistol into his pocket, then did a strange thing. He grabbed Will Harrison, hoisted the man to his shoulders and ran off with him as if he carried a bag of flour.

Slocum's hammer fell on an empty chamber. He cursed. There wasn't time to reload, even if he had a clean shot. With Harrison draped over the Indian's shoulders, any shot would be risky. Slocum skidded to a halt and looked into the cabin. His heart leaped into his throat.

Lying in the middle of the floor was the maharajah, bleeding profusely. The prince propped himself up on one elbow when he saw Slocum.

"Stop Ali. Kill him!"

"He's got Harrison," Slocum said, going into the cabin. He had to stop the bleeding from the three wounds in the maharajah's chest or the man would be dead soon. He used his knife to cut away the man's expensive silk shirt and sliced strips to bind the wounds. As he worked, the maharajah gasped out the story.

"I got here, talked to Will Harrison. He is going to return to India to see his father." The maharajah winced as Slocum tightened the bandage as tight as he could. "Ali, Ali the traitor! He and Valande were hired by Lawrence Harrison to kill Will."

"Who's Lawrence Harrison?"

"Robert and William's youngest brother."

Slocum understood then. The estate passed from the oldest to the next and on down. If the third brother were ever to inherit, both his older brothers had to be dead. Fighting in India had taken care of Robert, and Lawrence had somehow hired Ali and Valande to see to it that the maharajah never found William, and if they did, that he never lived long enough to enjoy his newfound position and wealth.

"Can you press in hard? There? Good. Let up and you might bleed to death. I've got to get you to a doctor."

"Save Will Harrison. You are not of my royal family, Mr. Slocum, but you should be bound by *rakhri* because of your dalliance with my sister." He held up the wrist with the braided bracelet. "Keep Ali from killing him. I will be all right."

Slocum saw that might be so. The wounds were gory, but now that the bleeding had been stanched, the maharajah might be all right if he didn't open the bullet holes again.

"Don't go digging in the mine for gold," Slocum said.

"I won't." The maharajah smiled weakly. "Will told me there is little gold to be found. This is a dry hole."

Slocum hastily reloaded and started for the door when the maharajah's command stopped him in his tracks.

"Be careful, Mr. Slocum. Return down the road. Ali had his horse in the ravine below the mine. If he follows that, it will take him longer to get to the valley where we left the elephant."

"I hope he won't kill Harrison out of hand," Slocum said.

"He needs proof that he has killed Will Harrison. I do not think he will assassinate him until he gets it."

"What proof?" Slocum saw the maharajah's strength fading as the man shrugged. Such details hardly mattered when overtaking the fleeing kidnapper and his victim counted more.

Slocum put his head down and began running at the fastest clip he thought he could maintain all the way downhill. He was tired from the climb to the mine, but the steep elevation worked in his favor now while Ali had to wind about some distance away. Slocum guessed the arroyo below Harrison's mine joined the larger arroyo where they had battled earlier.

Slocum stumbled several times but kept up his break-neck pace and reached the main road in less than half the time it had taken him to go up to the mine. He saw a startled Lakshmi look up from under a tree where she toyed with a mountain wildflower.

"What is it, John?"

"Your brother's shot up but is going to make it," he gasped out. "Ali's got Will Harrison. Ought to be along on horses anytime. Hear them?" Slocum tried to listen but the thunder of his own pulse drowned out softer sounds.

"Why, yes, horses whinnying." Lakshmi turned and pointed back down into the draw where Slocum suspected the arroyos merged. He was already running for the elephant, now standing and swaying slightly in the cool afternoon breeze. The animal's eyes popped open as Slocum approached. He swarmed up the rope circling the huge neck and settled himself so his feet rested behind the floppy ears.

"Giddy up, you gray behemoth," Slocum growled. He doubted the elephant understood but it began to walk—to run.

He was unable to control its speed as he turned it down the arroyo in the direction of the horses emerging from behind a curtain of tangled green vegetation that had overgrown the mouth of the gulch leading up to Harrison's mine.

Ali rode the white stallion and had Will Harrison draped over the saddle of another horse, the one Ali had ridden earlier. Slocum wasn't sure who was more surprised as the elephant charged headlong toward the men on the horses. He hardly knew that he reacted as he slid one leg over the elephant's head and then shoved off powerfully. Slocum sailed through the air and crashed hard into Ali, knocking the Indian servant to the ground.

Slocum rolled to his feet, drew his six-shooter and aimed it at Ali, but the man wasn't moving. He was knocked out cold.

"Whass that? El'phant?" came the wondering words from a battered Will Harrison. He flopped onto the ground and sat staring at the retreating hindquarters of the elephant as it continued its mad run down the arroyo and out of sight.

Slocum fingered his six-shooter as he stared down at Ali. The man had admitted to killing Hugh Malley, and that was as good a reason for shooting him as any. But Slocum jammed his six-gun back into its holster. Justice would be done, but there was someone else who ought to be there when Ali paid for his crime.

20

John Slocum was footsore by the time the small party made it back to Hoback Junction. The maharajah's injuries were such that he had to ride Slocum's horse. Slocum did not begrudge the prince the use of the white stallion—it had been his before he had given it to Slocum to replace a good horse that had been killed. Nor did he mind that Lakshmi rode with her brother. Will Harrison had ridden Ali's horse due to a broken leg he had sustained after Ali had dragged him from the shack down the rocky slope to the ravine where he had tethered the horses. Slocum didn't mind that all of them got to ride while he and Ali walked.

He liked the idea that Ali stumbled along, each step closer to town harder for the Indian to make because he knew what awaited him.

"There is the town," Lakshmi called from her high vantage point, but Slocum had already spotted the curls of smoke rising from half a hundred chimneys long since. "I'm sorry you have had to walk so many miles, John."

"There was no way I could catch the elephant," Slocum said, not sure if he was sorry about it at all. He had felt out of control every time he had climbed onto the elephant's neck to act as mahout. Still, the elephant was rampaging through the Grand Tetons with no one likely to capture it after the maharajah and his party left.

A slow smile came to Slocum's lips. The Crow Indians would have a fine meal if they could bring down the huge beast. It had enough meat on its bones to feed an entire Crow village throughout the winter. That would be the best outcome of letting the elephant charge up and down the valleys.

"That is all right, Mr. Slocum," said the maharajah. "The other one, a special elephant, ought to arrive soon. When it does, I can present it to Mr. Harrison and we can leave."

"I'm itchin' to get on back to India. Haven't been there in years," Will Harrison said. He had lost a great deal of his British accent during his time in the West, but enough remained that Slocum knew Harrison would regain it quickly. "Hate to think of my dear old dad dyin' like that."

"He is determined and will hang on to life until you arrive, William," the maharajah said.

"Might be so, but I have another problem. What do I do 'bout my little brother, Lawrence?"

Slocum knew what he would do to anyone hiring Ali and Valande to kill him, but he said nothing. This was something Will Harrison had to work out for himself, possibly with his father's consent. He doubted it was a unique situation since there were so many younger siblings of British lords. Not all of them lacked the ambition to take what their older brothers had, by hook or by crook.

"You get a statement from Ali before you leave," Slocum told the former remittance man. "I reckon he'll be willing to spill his guts in exchange for a lighter sentence."

"You will hang me," Ali said. "I am a dead man."

As he spoke, Slocum moved fast, coming up behind the Indian. Ali tried to bolt, hoping Slocum or the maharajah would gun him down. Slocum thrust out his foot and hooked it around Ali's, sending the man crashing facedown to the ground.

By now they were far enough inside Hoback Junction to draw a small crowd, including Marshal Rothbottom. Slocum had nothing but contempt for the lawman, but even Rothbottom had to agree to lock up Ali with so many witnesses against him. The confession made in front of Will, the maharajah and Slocum had to have some validity since it had been freely given, albeit in the heat of battle.

"We got ourselves a murderer, Marshal," Slocum said, pointing at the prone Ali. "He got that elephant of the maharajah's to stomp on Hugh Malley and kill him. There's a damn sight more but if you keep him locked up on that charge, we'll get around soon and give you a bigger list."

"Well, I dunno," said the marshal, chewing on his lower lip. "It's just you folks' say-so."

"It is on *my* say-so, Marshal," spoke up the maharajah. "My injuries are a result of being shot many times by Ali, my former servant and now my sworn enemy!" The prince ripped open his shirt and showed the bloody bandages Slocum had tied around his chest to bind up the bullet wounds. As the citizens saw the extent of the maharajah's injuries, a gasp went up. Slocum knew the bullet wounds looked worse than they were, but the dramatic moment and the response it got convinced the marshal to do something about Ali.

"Come on. I got a special cell waitin' fer ya," Rothbottom said, grabbing Ali by the collar and half dragging him along. "Reckon I kin keep ya locked up for destroyin' half my hoosegow."

"You need to get to the doctor," someone called from the boardwalk in front of the hotel. "Want me to go fetch him?"

"Do it," Slocum said, taking charge. He saw how pale the maharajah looked after his brief speech. "Look after

him, Lakshmi. And Mr. Harrison, you ought to tag along
and let the doc take a look at your gimpy leg."

"Thank you, Slocum," Will Harrison said. "We needed
someone to break the ice and get things movin' around
here. Thank you."

"Send me a bale of English pounds when you inherit the
Swansea estate," Slocum said. He knew how callous that
sounded and it didn't matter. He was tired of foot and soul.
But a curious lightness kept him moving along the main
street until he saw Darlene.

She stood outside the general store, a broom in her
hand. She tossed it aside and ran to him.

"John! You came back!"

"I brought Hugh's murderer in for trial," he told her. She
threw her arms around him and buried her face in his
shoulder. Darlene began sobbing. Her hot tears soaked into
his shirt.

"I didn't think you would, John. I doubted you. I'm
sorry. I'm so sorry."

Slocum had nothing to say to that. He held her awkwardly, not sure what to do until he looked down the street
and saw Lakshmi watching. Slocum tried to push Darlene
away, but she clung to him like a leech. Then he gave up
when it was apparent that Lakshmi saw nothing wrong in
comforting the woman.

Slocum had to admit to himself, also, that the time with
Lakshmi had been good—special. The princess was more
skilled between the sheets than most other women he had
come across in the West—not that he and Lakshmi had
ever found any sheets for their dalliances. Lakshmi gave a
special meaning to mysteries of the Orient, and Slocum
wished he had more time to explore them. But she was returning to India with her brother and Will Harrison. No
matter what had happened between them out on the trail, it
was over now. She was royalty, and he was nothing but a
saddle tramp.

That was fine with Slocum.

"Can we sit for a minute?" He pointed to chairs in front of the store. "Don't want to make your boss think you're falling down on the job."

"Mr. Benton's a nice old fellow," Darlene said, smiling a little now. "So what if he fires me? I've done what I had to do here. You're sure that Ali is the one who killed Hugh?"

"He admitted it in front of me, Will Harrison and the maharajah. I'll make sure the marshal doesn't forget to get statements from them before they leave." Slocum went on to explain how Harrison had come into a vast estate, or would when his father finally died.

"That's a shame," Darlene said. "That his brother died, I mean. Not that Mr. Harrison becoming rich is wrong. From all the gossip I've heard, that mine of his wasn't worth spit." She paused a moment, folded her hands in her lap and then said, "Why'd Ali kill Hugh? I don't understand."

"The maharajah was looking for a young man with a British accent. He had met Will Harrison more than ten years ago and, in spite of what he said, I don't think he believed he would actually recognize him when he found him. Being royalty and all, he didn't dare admit, even to himself, he might single out the wrong man."

"But Hugh was Welsh."

"I'll give the maharajah this much. I don't think he ever considered Hugh to be Will Harrison, but he might have thought Hugh could lead him to Harrison. Ali wanted to stop that at all costs. It didn't matter if Hugh actually was the heir to the Swansea title or might get the maharajah to the real heir."

"He was being paid by the third son to make sure no one found Will."

"And," Slocum went on, "if the maharajah did find him, to be sure that Will never claimed his title."

"Hugh died for nothing," Darlene said in a choked voice. She fought to hold back tears.

"Reckon so," Slocum said. There was no easy way to say it. Hugh Malley had been at the wrong place at the wrong time, and it had cost him his life.

Slocum turned when he heard a great commotion from down the street. He heaved a sigh of resignation when he saw an elephant swinging along, but this one was smaller than the one still roaming the Grand Tetons—and it was a peculiar dusty brown rather than gray.

"It's come!" shouted the maharajah.

Slocum and Darlene went into the street and joined the slow-moving prince and Lakshmi. Both Indians beamed with joy at seeing the elephant.

"This is the most special of elephants in existence," the maharajah said. "It is the rare white elephant."

"Don't look white to me," Darlene said.

"It's more of a title than description," Lakshmi explained. "But it is most rare and valuable."

"What are you going to do? Ride it back to India?" asked Slocum.

"It is yours, John Slocum, for all the valuable service you have given me. Of all Americans I have met, you are the best suited to riding like a maharajah!"

"I can't accept it," Slocum said, involuntarily taking a half step backward. "You said you were giving it to Harrison, as a gift."

"You cannot refuse," the maharajah said sternly. "It is a royal wish. That is the same as a command."

"Lakshmi said you weren't really a maharajah."

"I am yet a rajah, true. I can make such commands. Take possession of the white elephant, John Slocum. It is yours." The prince brooked no argument with his largesse.

"Oh, do, John," urged Darlene. "I have an idea."

"Thank you," Slocum said with ill grace. He touched the pocket where the huge diamond the maharajah had given him earlier still rested. At least he had gotten something of value. "You're letting me keep he stallion, aren't you?"

"That, also. You will be a well-traveled man, Mr. Slocum, on the finest of animals. Now we must go."

"Go?"

"Westward, over the Grand Tetons. Lakshmi has arranged for sea transport from San Francisco. I have horses to purchase and a party to form."

Slocum started to swap his services as a scout in exchange for taking back the white elephant, but Darlene elbowed him in the ribs.

"Let 'em go," she whispered.

Slocum knew she was right. It was hard enough to part with Lakshmi now. Spending another month on the trail with the woman would only make her departure in San Francisco all the more difficult.

"Have a safe trip. The mountains can be treacherous—and there's a rogue elephant on the loose out there."

The maharajah laughed and slapped Slocum on the back. Then he and Lakshmi left.

Slocum stared the white elephant in the eye but got no pleasure from the feeling that the elephant blinked first.

"I have a wonderful idea, John. There's a traveling circus in Cheyenne. If we get the elephant to them, I'm sure they'd buy it for a huge price."

"Think so?" Slocum stroked his chin. He could get the elephant across Wyoming in a week or two, find the circus, sell the elephant and split the money with Darlene. From Cheyenne it wasn't that far to Denver and diamond merchants who might give him a good price for the rock in his pocket.

And spending a couple more weeks with Darlene might not be so bad, either. He could teach her what he had learned from the *Kama Sutra*—and Lakshmi.

Watch for

SLOCUM AND THE SIERRA MADRAS GOLD

317th novel in the exciting SLOCUM series
from Jove

Coming in July!